The SATAN HUNTER

"Connie (Chung) and I have been working non-stop since we saw you . . . we could never have done it without your help and the support of the entire department."
Alexander Gleysteen
Producer, NBC News

"It was a pleasure to spend a day in your audience . . . . [it] was a UNIQUE EXPERIENCE!!! IT WAS EDUCATIONAL AS WELL AS INTERESTING. I don't know how many Forensic Dentists have taken your course but more of them should."
Curtis A. Mertz, D.D.S., Forensic Dental Consultant
Diplomate, American Board of Forensic Odontology

"I want to commend you for the excellent presentation . . . . We have heard nothing but favorable comments from those police officers present . . . . Apparently the type of activity you talked about is much more prevalent than anyone suspected."
Robert A. Malinowski, D.O.
Coroner's Office, County of Ashtabula, Ohio

"Tom has accurate knowledge, presents an interesting and informative program and is well prepared and is an excellent speaker."
Lt. John R. Loney
Clark County Sheriff's Dept.
Springfield, Ohio

"I would strongly recommend that church, civic, and social organizations give you the opportunity to share your materials with them."
Barry Stewart
Executive Producer
"New Directions"

The SATAN HUNTER

Thomas W. Wedge
with
Robert L. Powers

Calibre Press

Published by:

CALIBRE PRESS, INC.
666 Dundee Road
Suite1607
Northbrook, IL 60062-2760

PHONE: (800) 323-0037 or (708) 498-5680
FAX: (708) 498-6869

Fifth printing: April, 1992
First printing: October, 1988

Library of Congress Cataloging-in-Publication Data

Wedge, Thomas W., 1943-
  The satan hunter.
  Bibliography: p.
  Includes index.

    1. Satanism. 2. Cults. 3. Occult sciences.
    I. Powers, Robert L., 1933- . II. Title.
    BF1548.W43 1987   133.4′22   87-20219
    ISBN 0-935878-08-4

Printed in the United States of America

Dedication

"...We no longer could hear the screams from our brother officer. Finally, the order came to go into the house. Tear gas was lobbed into the three-bedroom home, followed by bursts from our automatic weapons. We tried to smash our way through the front door. Entry was difficult as the doors were barricaded with furniture. As we broke through the front door, the occupants began to fire at us from two different rooms, chanting and shouting as they fired.

"Just inside the front door we found him, or what was left of him. His hands were cuffed behind his back with his own handcuffs. His face was unrecognizable from the torture he had received. We became enraged. We went from room to room firing, until no one fired back.

"Afterward, as we examined our seven dead adversaries, one officer asked, 'What were they shouting?' Another responded, 'That we're the anti-Christ, agents of the Devil.' "

Memphis; January 13, 1983

This book is dedicated to all law enforcement officers who have died in the line of duty,

and

For Betty, whose love and encouragement made it possible.

"My people are destroyed for lack of knowledge . . ."

The Holy Bible
Hosea 4:5

Table of Contents

Acknowledgments

Special thanks to the following who made my book possible: Det. Dick Allen, Chris Black, Invest. Bill Buxton, Mary Lois Davis, Cheryl Eckhart, Dep. Ron Harwell, Sgt. Jessie Hughes, Dep. John V. Lala, Sgt. Thomas McCabe, Gary McLaughlin, Sheriff John G. Overly, Patricia Pulling, Officer Bruce Robb, Officer James Roepken, Jack M. Roper, Det. Fred S. Rounds, Det. Dave Spalding, Barry Stewart, Sheriff Milt Watts, Judge James B. West, Director Dan Willoby, and to the many others who have contributed to this book with their knowledge and expertise.

1

Sean Sellers

Did Satan's demons cause a 16-year-old worshipper to brutally kill his parents? Sean Sellers says that's exactly what happened to him. He has been found guilty of those murders, as well as the death of a convenience store clerk. Today, at 17, he has been sentenced to die by lethal injection for those crimes.

The tragedy of Sean Sellers, a handsome and bright young man, is perhaps the best-known case involving the growing national problem of Satanic worship. It is a story difficult to pinpoint because of alleged attempts by the nation's media to downplay stories about Satan worshippers in an attempt to "prevent panic."

I have been working as an investigator of the occult for nearly a dozen years. I was summoned by Sellers' defense attorneys to testify as an expert witness at the high school student's murder trial in Oklahoma City, Okla., during the summer of 1986. Sellers granted me a lengthy exclusive interview from his prison cell. He frankly discussed his relationship with the Devil and how that "friendship" led to the deaths of three people, including Sean's mother and stepfather.

Several months after Sean was convicted of these killings, he telephoned me one night and gave a detailed confession of his crimes. That confession is revealed at the end of this chapter.

Sean gives every appearance of a typical, clean-cut young Midwesterner. He's tall, slender, well-groomed.

Sean keeps his hair short and neatly combed; he wears no jewelry. He appears to be the epitome of the All American Boy.

In a television appearance from prison in McAlester, Okla., on the nationally-syndicated "Oprah Winfrey Show," Sean spoke with seeming sincerity and a marked politeness. He failed to rise to the occasion as the talk show host attempted to discredit his words. She made little effort to conceal an apparent disgust with his actions.

The young man's involvement with the occult and supernatural began when he was in the third grade.

"It kept going from there," he told me calmly as we sat together in the spartan, barred interview room. Sean demonstrates intelligence. His speech patterns show no evidence of grammatical disasters. His dark eyes search out his interviewer. He says he has found God and that he has become "born again." He speaks of remorse and how he hopes to put his life in order, to become an example to other young people and to warn of the danger of involvement with the occult, the horrors that await those who dare to dabble with the unknown.

"As I got older, I became heavily involved in Dungeons and Dragons." D&D is a complicated game which conservatives and fundamentalist Christians often accuse of being laced with heavy doses of Satanism. The game, its opponents claim, causes players to lose contact with reality as they become entranced with its machinations, twists and turns.

Sellers admits that his ties to Satanic worship gathered strength as the years passed. Interviewed by Oklahoma City news media after his arrest, he said that he would advise other people to "stay away from Satanism and the occult."

His advice: "Get involved with religion." He now professes "a close relationship with God."

Sellers was arrested following a telephone tip to police. When authorities searched his room, they uncovered copies of three books that he admitted using in Satanic worship. They were: *"The Satanic Bible,"* by self-proclaimed High Priest of The Church of Satan, Anton Szandor LaVey, *"The Satanic Rituals,"* also authored by LaVey, and another ritual volume called the *Necronomicon*. The books all are published in inexpensive paperback editions by Avon Books of New York and have been steady sellers for nearly two decades. "The Satanic Bible" was first marketed in 1969, and has gone through at least 21 printings.

As Sellers began to absorb those manuals, he intertwined his beliefs in Satanism with the study of martial arts, especially the Ninja variation of that creed.

During the interview, I asked Sean if he ever had sacrificed any animals.

"No, because I love animals," he said.

"But in being a Satanist," I argued, "blood sacrifices are required."

"I used my own blood," he said, pointing to a scar on one of his arms. He adds that he had worked at a clinic and stole hypodermic needles and used those to extract his own blood.

Involvement with the coven, where he says his coven name was "The Eliminator," went much deeper than was brought out in court testimony during Sellers' trial. The young man had entered into a blood pact, a copy of which was introduced during his trial. "I renounce God; I renounce Christ; I will serve only Satan. To my enemies, death; to my friends

13

love. Hail, Satan." The inscription was written in blood and signed by Sellers.

When a Satanist renounces God and Christ, the renunciation of Christ is the more important of the two. In order to reach God, a Satanist believes he must go through His Son. In a coven initiation, one of the initial rituals demanded is the renunciation of Christ.

A Satanist always believes in God. Satanism requires a mocking of the principals of Christianity, thereby requiring that its adherents believe in God, while rejecting all He represents.

Another document uncovered during the trial was a note Sellers had written in a Satanic alphabet, scribbled in his blood. When deciphered, the message said, "I am a son of Satan. Satan is forever my lord."

The initial pacts with Satan had been made. Sellers had pledged his body and mind to Satan.

Sellers had claimed during initial questioning by police that he did not kill the convenience store clerk. He then blamed a companion for the slaying, while admitting that he had been present.

He says that his friend asked him, "How can you be a Satanist and never have killed anyone?" For a long time, and during the time of his trial, Sean asserted that he could not remember murdering his parents. "I wish I could remember if I really did it," he said. But that story changed. For several months he was interviewed by Civia Tamarkin, Chicago-based reporter for *People Weekly*, and he told Tamarkin that he had denied the killing even to himself. In his trial, he was silent. His attorneys entered a plea of not guilty. He told them that he couldn't remember committing the crimes, but he told the lawyers of his infatuation with the Devil. They told the court that Sellers' relationship with Satan had made him insane.

The jury didn't buy his story. He was found guilty on all three counts. One juror was quoted by *People*: "If that verdict saves one kid from Satanism, or saves one other person from getting killed, then it's justified."

After the trial, Sellers came to realize what he had done. "I'm having a hard time dealing with the guilt, but I have to tell the truth about what Satanism can do," he told Tamarkin.

Sellers claims that he had been using amphetamines for "a couple of days," at the time his parents were slain; however "speed" usually does not cause a person to become violent.

Witnesses who saw Sellers come out of his parents' home after their murders said that he was "as white as a ghost." They said he muttered, "My parents are dead."

In my interview, I asked Sellers when he had last worshiped the devil. Police had discovered an altar in his home. On that altar rested an athame, a knife used in Satanic rituals, as well as silver chalices. In my hours with the young man, I tried to ask him qualifying questions, answers to which would normally be known only by a practicing, devout Satan worshipper. He provided correct answers.

"Why did you use silver chalices?" I asked.

He didn't hesitate in his answer. "Gold symbolizes the purity of Christianity, while silver is, in Satanism, the opposite of Christianity."

He also had ceremonial swords, and an old piece of carpet used as a prayer cloth. He possessed incense oils that he burned during worship. The elaborate altar was set up in his room.

"I last worshipped Satan the night before my parents were killed," he says.

I asked him about his use of the pentagram, a five-pointed star surrounded by a circle that is used by worshippers as a protection against demons conjured during services. The star is inverted. The two upward points represent Satan and the Antichrist, while the three downward points signify the Father, Son and Holy Spirit, the members of the Christian Trinity.

By having the two points on top, Satanists believe this signifies dominance of the Devil over Christianity. The circle means protection is offered.

In most cases, the pentagram is drawn on the floor. But covens often vary in their use of a pentagram. In Sean's case, he chose to draw the pentagram on his chest, in his own blood. He added that he "felt sorry" for the demonic forces he was trying to summon.

"I scrubbed the pentagram from my chest," he says. "I asked the demonic forces to enter my body and use me as they wished."

When I was called by Sellers' defense attorneys as an expert witness in his murder trial, I testified that I did not believe that he was in a coven by himself. I think there was more involvement than has been uncovered.

When he washed off that pentagram, I believe he opened himself to a form of demon possession and not the Hollywood type. There's no spitting of green pea soup or the 360-degree twisting of the head.

According to the Bible, one of the archangels who was cast out of Heaven by God was Lucifer, another name for the Devil or Satan. He was a top-ranking archangel. Because of his pride, he was sent away from heaven. One third of the angel population at that time chose to follow Lucifer, or Satan.

When one discusses demons or dark forces, we refer to that one-third of the angel population who decided to follow Satan. Not knowing the exact size of the angel population, there can be no way of determining the size of the one-third who left.

I believe that those who begin to dabble in Satanism, in their conjurations and summons, actually summon up the demonic forces. As time passes, Satan's worshippers study and gain more knowledge about their "religion." Thus, they are able to call up more dangerous demonic forces.

In Sean Sellers' case, I think that when he removed his

16

protection (the pentagram) and prayed for the demonic forces to enter him, he called up forces that used him. For a long time, Sellers claimed not to remember killing his parents because of the influence of those forces. The jurors were not convinced. One said, "We thought he knew right from wrong."

It has become common for those accused of murder to use the defense that they were under the influence of a drug, such as heroin. By claiming diminished capacity, they think they should be found innocent by jurors. But when one enters a courtroom and pleads the defense that Sean Sellers attempted to use, testifying about spiritual warfare and demonic forces, jurors do not want to listen. They refuse to believe that such might be true.

It seems apparent that Sean did not enter Satanism of his own accord. He was recruited; there are recruiters who look for susceptible persons. I testified during the Sellers trial that there is an organization called the Abbey, a society founded by Aleister Crowley in 1920. There is an Abbey in Oklahoma City, which I believe is a recruitment house for young people such as Sean. He told me that he possessed a ring which was given to him by a person who placed it on his finger. This man claimed to have been involved in the occult for approximately 18 months.

Recruiters go to extensive lengths to find persons who might be interested in becoming involved. Sean was recruited through information gained from his girlfriend, a 15-year-old called, ironically, Angel.

This girl was being educated by the other person to become a Satanist. She divulged information to the recruiter, who then was able to use that information in his recruiting of Sean.

Recruiters will trick youngsters into joining by such methods as drawing a pentagram on their forehead or in the palm of a hand with a bar of soap. When this area is dampened, the recruiter then can apply cigarette ashes, causing the previously invisible pentagram to mysteriously appear.

Recruiters did their homework on Sean. People who professed to be his friends went on the stand during his trial and testified against him.

A young man, who must be labeled an accomplice, allegedly accompanied Sean when he went to the Circle K convenience store on March 1, 1985. At Sean's trial, this person testified against Sean, claiming that Sellers had killed the clerk at the store. The witness also described how Sellers murdered his parents.

Sean told me that he has accepted Jesus Christ as his Saviour and that "I am willing to accept the consequences of whatever I may have done." Even if that means death by lethal injection, Sean says he will accept it. During our conversations, other topics were covered. Sean displayed considerable knowledge of the subject of Satanism. In addition to his collection of commercially-available books, he had made his own "Book of Shadows." Sean also was corresponding with a friend in Colorado, seeking a coven that he might join. He spoke of other teachers in the Oklahoma City area that "are gone; they no longer can be found." He told me of the Enochian Chain, the Enochian Language.

As I testified during Sean's trial, I realized this case was much more complicated than anyone realized. This was not an instance of a single young individual, acting upon his own. It rather was a case of numerous individuals deeply involved, influencing a lonely, frustrated young man. Sean had no self-esteem. He was unquestionably led by a group that I believe still exists. It is a group that operates today, in secret. It is putting other young people into peril. That group's membership is minus one: Sean Sellers sits on Death Row in a maximum security prison, awaiting the court wrangling and appeals process that could ultimately lead to his execution, once all avenues are exhausted.

It is my hope that, through the information I am providing

18

in the pages of this book, I can prevent another Sean Sellers case from occurring, that I can keep another youngster from being enticed into the cruel, deadly world of Satanism.

In one of Sean's writings, he says, "Right now, I need some blood. I've got a craving for blood. I don't work at the clinic anymore. Maybe I can buy some from the hospital. I think I'll try. Man, I want to drink blood so badly."

In another excerpt from his writings, he talks about a place in Oklahoma City called the Abbey. "It is a school," Sean wrote, "a cult for magic. I know a guy there who's going to teach me magic." Sean told me that he knows a girl who is receiving instruction from the Abbey, but he refused to give me its location.

"There also are people at the school who wish to get introduced," he wrote. "I know about another group, and I know where they meet. I'm going to find them out there pretty soon."

Sean was writing about covens. He discusses the girl who introduced him to the man who turned over his ring to Sean. Through her interrogation of Sean, this girl obtained information about Sean which she gave to the teacher in this "school for magic."

One of the people who testified for the prosecution in the Sellers trial claimed to have been a wizard, which in the *Satanic Dictionary* is defined as a male witch. He told the jury that he had lied "so many times that he wanted to take the stand and tell the truth." He wore a cross in one of his pierced ears.

He said that he had "made up" different stories to recruit people. He had worked as a security guard at showings of the popular cult film, "The Rocky Horror Picture Show," which has attracted hundreds of thousands of costumed fans to midnight shows in theaters across the country for the past decade.

What better place could there be for a recruiter working

for Satan than at theaters showing this film?

This young man who slipped his ring onto Sean's finger claimed that he was able to teach Sean "magical powers" and had made many claims about Satanism. When he testified, he spoke of his lies about all this.

I think he was exactly who he said he was. He was using recruiting techniques that are common for Satan's followers.

Ironically, when Sean was being questioned by police concerning the deaths of his parents, an anonymous phone call was received at police headquarters. The caller told authorities that Sean had committed the murder at the Circle K store.

The individual who turned state's evidence and is now a free man, allegedly had been Sean's "best friend." According to Sean, the man actually was an accomplice to the crime at the convenience store.

When this man went to the police, he told them that Sean had confessed details in the murder of the Circle K employee and then told him fully about how he (Sean) had slain his parents.

The question must be raised as to why this informant waited for six months after the Circle K murder before going to authorities to tell them about Sellers' alleged confessions.

In writings Sean composed before his parents' deaths, he made an obvious cry for help. Sean's mother had gone to a church and showed the minister the materials about Satanism that she had found in Sean's room. She was told that she had no right to meddle in Sean's affairs and that she should return the materials to her son.

Sean's IQ is 118. Psychologists offered varying testimony on his state of mind.

Psychologist Martin Krimsky said, "If Sean killed his parents, his body acted but his mind registered nothing. Physically he was acting in a integrated manner. Mentally he was not aware, not appreciating, not registering what was happening."

In other words, Sean Sellers was not in total control of his own mind. He was worshipping Satan. When he went before the altar the night before he killed his parents, he had no protection on him. He invited demonic forces to come into his body. They did. Those forces took control of him.

Few, if any, secular psychologists would be willing to testify in a court trial and admit that they believe in demonic forces. That carries this case, as well as many others, into the realm of religion. Anyone who believes in God must, it follows, believe in Satan. And if one believes in Satan, then that person must believe in fallen angels. Fallen angels are the demonic forces.

There's no problem for most people in talking about guardian angels. But when demons — or fallen angels — are mentioned, then there's a problem. Sean claimed to have loved his parents. They had the usual up-and-down relationship that is common to all of us. But there is no evidence anywhere in Sean's writings that he held an opinion of his parents that would cause him to hate them enough to kill them. Never does Sean indicate that he hated his parents.

He had the normal, everyday problems common to a 16-year-old and his parents.

Here is a letter Sean wrote to his parents. This letter was taken from a clipboard in his parents' living room:

"Mom and Dad:

"I may be dumb, but I thought about it and I'm just going to have to go for it. I took everything I could find that was mine, except for the bed and Toughie. I'll be by tomorrow or so to get them. I didn't leave because I don't love you or because I'm mad at you, but because I want to try it on my own for a change. I don't want it to be as if I was kicked out, or as if I have run away. I'd still like to visit and keep in touch, but if that answer is no, I understand. I'll be back or I'll be at work until 11 o'clock and then I've got some things to organize. Since I've already driven the pickup around, I went ahead and took it to work, I'll see you tomorrow and explain how I'm planning on working things out.

"Love always,

"Sean."

What happens when young people get involved in Satanism? When they obtain a copy of *"The Satanic Bible?"*

These are writings from Sean:

"In *The Satanic Bible*, there are four books: *The Book of Satan, The Book of Lucifer, The Book of Belial* and *The Book of Leviathan*. Each name is a power of Hell. Before crown princesses of Hell, Satan, Hebrew, adversary, opposite accuser, Lord of the Flies, Inferno, and represents the South. Lucifer which is Roman, the bringer of light, enlightenment, the morning star and represents the east.

Sean mentioned that he is Hebrew, without a master, independent, and he is something of the earth and represents the north. Leviathan. Each name represents a different element and a different destination. Earth, water, fire, air, east, west, south, north.

"In Satanism, one's birthday is the most important holiday of the year. Walpurg is is the night celebrated on the eve of May 1, Halloween or rather Happy Halloween. The summer solstice, which is in June, the winter equinox which is in December, the spring equinox in March and the autumn equinox in September.

"God f---'s chickens. All of these holidays are around the 21st or the 22nd of decided months. During each holiday, a witch's power is increased for that night. Also, once a year there is a black mass in which you have the biggest meeting of that year. I think this is when humans may be sacrificed. If you don't outrage a lot of people, then the holiday is no good. Sacrificed people are those people who beat their wives, molest children, kick their dogs, etc. We do the world a favor by getting rid of them. After all, people like this have no right to live, anyway. Among witches and Satanists, suicide is an

22

ultimate no-no."

Sean goes on to speak about the white witches' only true powers, which are those used to heal others. "Black magic is the only way," he writes.

"To become a witch, you have to be devoted to Satan and witchcraft. Remember, this is black magic and to get that power which you so crave, Lucifer is the only way. When you make up your mind for good, I'll send you some stuff to really get started. I don't think you really understand what worshipping Satan means. Perhaps these will help you.

"These are the nine Satanic statements:

"1. Satan represents indulgence, instead of abstinence!

"2. Satan represents vital existence, instead of spiritual pipe dreams!

"3. Satan represents undefiled wisdom, instead of hypocritical self-deceit!

"4. Satan represents kindness to those who deserve it, instead of love wasted on ingrates!

"5. Satan represents vengeance, instead of turning the other cheek!

"6. Satan represents reponsibility to the responsible, instead of concern for psychic vampires!

"7. Satan represents man as just another animal, sometimes better, more often worse than those that walk on all-fours, who, because of his 'divine spiritual and intellectual development,' has become the most vicious animal of all!

"8. Satan represents all of the so-called sins, as they all lead to physical, mental, or emotional gratification!

"9. Satan has been the best friend the church has ever had, as he has kept it in business all these years!

(This material was copied from *The Satanic Bible*, page 25; Copyright 1969 by Anton Szandor LaVey.)

"Look over these, and reread them until you understand each one of them. If you agree with them, then you'll be ready to devote, if you don't agree, then witchcraft isn't for you after all. It's wonderful. You wouldn't believe how it really feels. Write down info and burn.

"Go over them and maybe you'll see what I mean. I wish I could talk to you and tell you about some of this stuff; but until you are sure you want to get as deep into this as I am, you're just going to have to wait. Last night during my prayers, I cut the hell out of myself with my knife. It cut pretty deep. You can even see the meat between the skin, but blood never ran from it. Now is that weird? Pretty soon, I think I'll be able to encounter a demon and I might be able to get my new name. Later on, I might be able to tell you about Melissa. She's so neat. Write me back really soon, like today, so I can get you more things. I haven't got your letter, so I've sent these two. Whatever you want to know, ask me and I'll try to find out. Remember not to tell anyone about all of this. Christians seem to look down upon Satanists for some reason. I wonder why. Yes, I may be becoming evil, but I'm proud of it. All of this may never change me, so don't start worrying, I've just got a new outlook on life, and it says, "Hail, Satan." The totally evil is still lovable. (Signed) Sean."

In another letter, talking about a trip Sean plans to make, he writes:

"Probably on the first night, we'll make our sacrifice and hold our ritual of undertaking. Undertaking of the job which I am going to explain. In the book of the Satanic rituals, Mr. LaVey said that we have just come out of the world of an age of ice in which God is above. Now the age of fire is upon us. The ages of fire and ice rotate every thousand years or so and the new age of fire started in 1966. That is why The Satanic Church was built, an age of fire. God is beneath and Satan is above.

"There was a child born in 1966. He was 18 in 1984 and in the year 2002 he will rise into power. This child may be the Antichrist, the son of Satan himself. If he isn't, then he still is someone who will have very much power. I have been given the option to help Lucifer rise to power helping Satanism become the dominant religion on earth. One Satanist equals ten Christians in Power. Can you imagine a world dominated with our kind? If I accept this job, I will have more power than you can imagine. I want you to help me, be my partner. If you do, when we die, we shall be rulers of supreme power under very few-over nearly all in Hell. Will you join me in my task? Think about it.

"P.S. Included is the most powerful symbol of Satan. (A pentagram.)"

In another letter:

"God's name is Jehovah. Our god's name is Satan. But our god is just a little like a president or teacher. While Satan has many names, Lucifer is probably the most known, besides Satan. I'm going to warn you that you'll suffer the consequences when spelling Satan. Always use a big "S". Remember, in order to get power from Satan you must earn his respect and prove yourself to him. Satan rules the earth today. Evil, Sean."

"P.S. I love you like a brother, but not like a sister."

On November 13, 1986, Sean Sellers called me collect from McAlester Prison Death Row. This is the story he told me of the store clerk's murder:

Sean and his friend Richard were at Sean's house. Sean's cousin was there. They performed a lust ritual for Richard, outside. They then went back into the house and started talking about killing Tracy's father — Tracy is Richard's girlfriend, now his wife.

Sean said, "It's too bad we don't have a gun." Richard then obtained his grandfather's revolver, as well as an old .22 caliber rifle. They found shells for both, Sean added. He said they had planned on driving to a Circle K store, to rob and kill the person who was cashier there. The man who worked at the Circle K store had refused to sell beer to Sean and Richard on a previous night. The employee at the store also had allegedly flirted with Tracy when she purchased tampons. After robbing the store and murdering the employee, they planned to go to Tracy's house and knock out Jeremiah and kill her parents.

Before leaving the house, Sean told me, "We dedicated the next few hours to Satan." They left the house. In their car, they prayed to Satan to give Sean strength and to take the sacrifice, using the incantation "Izoin Kathenthea Coinsea," I asked Sean what this meant. He said Melissa, who was involved in the occult and Satanism, taught him that this incantation involved all his demons. He said this incantation "opened the portal holes for all the demonic forces."

Sean said that when they arrived at the Circle K, they talked to the clerk for almost an hour. Richard lured him outside and had the man look at the clutch on the car. Richard and the employee compared clutches in their cars, Sean said. Richard showed the man his stereo, trying to distract him. Richard and the man went back inside.

Sean was in the passenger seat of Richard's car, sitting on a .357 Magnum revolver. Richard said, "OK," and Sean walked around to the dark side of the store. "I thought I had lost my nerve," Sean said.

Sean walked into the store. "I will never forget how I felt," he said. "I was calm. There was no hate, only pure evil."

Sean said, "I had felt like this before, but never like that night."

Richard had the employee distracted in the back of the store. The clerk was behind the counter, with his eyes on Richard. He was drinking a cup of coffee.

Sean said, "I picked up the gun, raised it and fired. I missed him. He dropped his coffee, raised his hand up about elbow height, and started saying, 'OK, man; all right.' He was terrified." Sean said the man started to go to the cash register. "I kept the gun on him," he added. Sean continued, "I looked at him and he realized that I was going to kill him. He knew us and thought we were going to rob him. He could turn us in."

Then Sean said that the employee looked in Sean's eyes. "He looked into my eyes and saw that I was going to kill him." At this point, Richard walked forward from the back of the store. The clerk started to run toward the restroom. "He slipped and fell. I lowered the gun and fired again." That was the second shot.

"The man kind of screamed. I thought I hit him. He got back up and kept running in the direction he had been going. Richard got in his way. He was ducking down, bent over and ran back toward the cash register. Richard crossed behind me and I went back around where the man had fallen. He then ran back toward me. When he looked up, he saw me. I was right up on him, and Richard said, 'Do it.' I fired and the guy fell. Blood went everywhere. The first shot missed. The second shot hit him in the area of the neck. The third shot hit him in the side. I turned around. Richard was draped over the counter, trying to figure which button to push to open the cash register. I said, 'Go. Go.' He took off, running out the door."

Sean said he ran behind Richard and he got in the car and drove away.

"We had wasted too many bullets at the Circle K, so we didn't go to Tracy's house, because we thought the gun could be easily traced back to us."

When I asked Sean if the man at the Circle K was a human sacrifice, Sean answered, "The man at the Circle K, in technical terms, was a sacrifice to Satan."

Sean added that the next morning, "I didn't remember what had been done. Richard did, but I was not sure. The night before we had wiped off the gun and put it back in the case where Richard's grandfather had kept it. Richard took the two bullets not used and did something with them. I took the three empty shells and went in Richard's backyard, where I buried them,"

27

Sean then said he stayed at Richard's house all night. "We talked about what happened. We laughed about it, because the poor guy was terrified. He never suspected being killed."

Sean said he went on about his normal business the next day. He and Richard drove past the Circle K store and saw "a lot of cop cars." They drove on to another Circle K outlet and inquired what had happened. They were told that a man had been shot to death.

At that point, Sean said, he "kind of remembered going to the Circle K and I was thinking, wow, we were there right before it happened; this guy was killed." The two went about their normal activities.

Richard was charged with being an accessory to the murder, but when he turned state's evidence, he was given several years' probation. That killing occurred Sept. 8, 1985. Sean's mother and stepfather were killed on March 5, 1986.

His mother was Vonda Maxine Bellofatto, 32; his stepfather was Paul Leon Bellofatto, 43. Both were found shot to death in their waterbed at their duplex, 7139 Northwest 115th Street in Oklahoma City.

Sean said, "I worshipped that night at my altar, which was set up against the wall facing my mother and dad's bedroom. I remember performing a ritual, summoning the demons, asking them to enter my body." He ended the ritual and went to bed.

From that point, "it was sort of like a dream. I got out of my bed, wearing my black underwear. I had the gun in my room. It was a .44 Magnum. I laid a towel down in the hall, along with a holster, without the gun in it."

He said he walked into the bedroom, and "I shot them." I asked him, who did you shoot? "My dad. I shot him in the head. I pulled the trigger, I then lifted the gun a couple of inches and pulled the trigger again. My mother raised her head a little bit, so I fired again. I then walked out of the room, put the gun in the holster and wrapped it in the towel.

I took a shower, came out and got dressed. When I did my ritual, I put on a pair of black underwear and a black, hooded cape.

"After my shower, I went back into my mom and dad's bedroom and turned on the light and looked at them. I was very proud of myself. I kind of laughed and I was very calm at all times. He said, "I felt really good. I felt like a big burden had just been lifted off my shoulders, because they had interfered with my girl and with my practice of Satanism."

Sean then said that he put on his coat, got the gun and bullets. He had wiped off prints in the house. He went to his pickup truck and drove around, finally going to a friend's home (Richard). "Richard came out and I told him that my mom and dad were dead."

"Richard said, 'You did it?' and I said, 'Yes,' Richard laughed and said, 'Good.' "

Sean said that his friend "got real cold. He was ecstatic about it." He said they went back into the house, then returned to turn off the lights in Richard's car. When they went back to the house, Richard wanted details about the murders.

Sean said Richard told him that he had dreamed about Sean's actions. "He told me how my father was lying in bed, and where I was standing. He was accurate. At this point, it got foggy and I can't remember what was said."

He said he obtained his briefcase from the pickup. He said the briefcase contained "all my Satanic things," including the *Book of Shadows, Satanic Bible,* the *Necronomicon,* etc.

"I then spent the night at Richard's home. The next morning I got up like nothing was wrong. Because I had overslept, I was late for school." He said he drove back to his parents' home to get a note from his parents. He found them, "and my reaction was like wow! When I first saw them it was like something inside of me switched on and I freaked out and started crying. I yelled and ran next door and had them call an ambulance."

29

He said Richard pushed him outside the house, where he tripped and fell over a bush. "I just started crying." He said that Tracy, Richard's girlfriend, came over and put her arms around him. A man who lived across the street arrived.

At this point in the conversation, I asked Sean whether, on the night he shot his parents, he was wearing a pentagram or any sort of protection from demons. He responded, "No."

"Did you ask the demons to come into you?" I asked him. "Were they present?"

He answered, "Every time I would ask demons to enter me, I would feel chilled and my chest would expand." He said the demon was called Ezurate. I asked where the name came from. He said that when he had first begun to invoke demons, "It came to me."

"Have you ever seen them?" I asked. He said no. But he said the demons had spoken to him. Once when he was taking a vocabulary test at school, he had not studied. "I made a 98 and I hadn't studied at all."

Later, I received a phone call from Civia Tamarkin, Chicago bureau reporter for *People Weekly*, who told me she had received a call from Sean and that he had confessed to the Circle K killing as well as the murder of his mother and stepfather. Sean told her that he committed the murder because he had broken every one of the ten commandments except for murder. He also said that he had been on "speed" for three days.

Most of his report to Tamarkin coincided with the information he gave me.

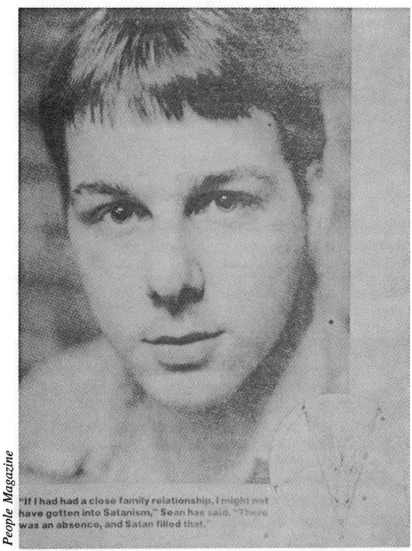

Sellers is now on death row in McAlester Prison where he has been sentenced to die by lethal injection for the murder of a convenience store clerk and his mother and stepfather. After Sean accepted Jesus Christ as his Saviour, he called Tom Wedge and told him the story that started at an altar set up to worship Satan in his bedroom and ending in a small cell on death row at McAlester Prison.

People Magazine

Sean Sellers at age 17 on death row. In a letter he told Tom Wedge that he never thought a year ago that he would be on death row waiting to die. He told Wedge in the letter to read a special letter to those who he speaks to. The letter is a very special one that tells all of those who are searching to avoid anything that deals with the occult.

Tom Wedge and NBC's Connie Chung. Wedge acted as a consultant during a taping dealing with satanism that aired on NBC and was hosted by Connie Chung and Roger Mudd. Wedge is one of the leading experts on satanism in the United States.

My dear friends,

I sit here at a steel desk in a cell on death
row in Oklahoma. I'm 17 years old. When
I close my eyes I imagine the faces of all who
hear this letter. I see faces just like mine
less than a year ago. Faces full of confusion
and often pain. Faces searching for something.
I was there too. I was looking for a place
to fit in just like you. I found that place, before
an alter of Satan. I let an interest in Dungeons
and Dragons become an obsession that later
led me into Sataniam. I performed rituals covered
in blood, inviting demons to enter my body.
I drank blood, sometimes mixed with wine and
urine, and began taking drugs. I thought I had
at last found what I was looking for. I was
wrong. Now as a result of all I did in Satanism
I am condemned to die.
My friends, I am not an adult, I'm a teenager.
I know what it's like out there and very often
it's not easy, but look where I am, it can always
get worse. Many people can tell you many
things, but it's your decision to listen. I pray
you will listen to me. I'm just not a speaker
on a platform, I'm not a preacher but I am
a teenager.
I followed the ways of society, the ways of
uncaring, of immorality, of rebellion. I looked
to drugs, alcohol, and Satanism for answers
to my problems. I never just stopped to look
around me.
Walk outside and look at the sky, at the trees,
the ground, the flowers. Just look around you
and see the clouds, the birds, the sunshine.
Can't you see the awesome love of the One who
created all this for you? You know, drugs,
alcohol, the occult, that all seems to cool; are
you too cool to see that Jesus loves you? I
was, and now where am I?
No, my friends, drugs, alcohol, the occult,
all that trash, they're not answers to problems.
Every day teens kill themselves because everyone
around them was too cool to tell them about
Jesus, or because they also turned to these
for answers instead of turning to the only real
answer. All these are not answers, they're
only more problems disguised as answers. Jesus
is the only answer.

Where are you headed? When people look
at you what do they see? Do they see a person
too cool to stop and talk to about their problems?
Do they see a person full of rebellion? If
they do, you could end up as I have. Or do
they see a person who really cares, a person
who is really cool?

I never knew what it was to live until
someone told me I had to die. What will it
take for you? You could make such a difference
in your own life, and so many others as well.
Listen to me. You can see where I am. I
followed the ways of society. I fell into the
traps of the devil. Make a stand in your life,
learn to care for one another, learn to love
one another and teach others to do the same.
Jesus is the only way. I know. He loves you
more than you ever can imagine. Won't you
give Him a fair chance in your life? Just
give Jesus a fair chance in your life.

There are people who care Never think
that no one cares, because I do. I care because
I love you. I love you because Jesus loves
you, and if you're good enough for Him, then
you're good enough for me. It took a long
time to learn to say those words. How long
will it take you? I had to go through hell
to learn something so simple. Will you let
me teach you? I love you my friends.

Forever in Christ,

Sean

ABOUT THIS LETTER:
Sean wrote this personal letter
to Tom Wedge to read to the many
thousands of young adults he
speaks to across the United
States.

Sean Sellers
156641
P.O. Box 97
McAlester, OK 74501

2

Position and Fall of Satan

In Isaiah 14:12-14, Lucifer is labeled the highest among the angelic creatures. The Bible says that he was annointed for a position of great authority. According to Ezekial 28:12-15, Lucifer was created with perfect wisdom and perfect beauty.

The name Lucifer itself means Day Star, Light Bearer or Son of the Morning. Lucifer met with God's disfavor after he expressed the five "I Wills," as found in Isaiah. They are as follows: I will ascend into Heaven, I will exalt my throne above the stars of God; I will sit also among the mount of the congregation; I will ascend above the heights of the clouds; and I will be like the most high.

Because of Lucifer's pride, he underwent a change of name to Satanas, which means adversary, and was removed from the high position of archangel. Not only did he fall, the Bible reports, but one-third of the existing angels chose to follow him.

In Jude 6, the Bible says that the angelic beings were cast

out of heaven into the air. This is why Satan is sometimes referred to as the Prince of the Power of the Air. This reference appears in Ephesians 2:2.

Not enough has been said about Satan. The facts that must be driven home are that he was a created being, that he was an archangel who sat at the throne of God, and that because of the pride and greed that entered into his life, he made the choice to try to become like God. By so doing, he lost his position as one of God's own. Satan was cast out.

For anyone reading this book, the point cannot be overemphasized that Satanists or Satanic cults have an extremely powerful influence. It is extremely important that one realize that Satanists believe wholeheartedly in the existence of one Satan. Their faith in such an entity makes any cultist dangerous and not to be taken lightly.

Satanists believe that their leader will recapture the throne that he lost.

SACRIFICES

In Genesis 31:54, the Bible states that Jacob offered a sacrifice on the mountain and called his kinsmen to a meal, which they consumed.

There are numerous passages in the Bible that deal with animal sacrifices, as well as other sacrifices. In Biblical times, sacrifices would be offered to Jehovah. Non-traditional Satanists, in most cases, kill an animal and just leave the remains, usually mutilating the animal and taking only the desired parts.

The ultimate sacrifice, of course, was Jesus Christ. He became the sins of the world; He became the Lamb; He became the One who shed His blood.

Christians believe that Jesus took the sins of the world on His shoulders that day and bore those sins when He was crucified and His blood was shed for those sins. Through Jesus' crucifixion and resurrection, the unsaved person is given the opportunity to accept Jesus Christ as a personal saviour. When an individual accepts Jesus, God forgives him of his sins, no matter what they might be. The saved one becomes "a child of God."

The Scriptures say that the only route to the Father is through His Son. Without knowing the Son, one can never know the Father.

The point is that in Satanism, the blood, the sacrifices, all the different rituals, have a religious flavor. All the things Satanists do constitute blasphemies against the Christian religion. Satanists mock Christianity.

In order to comprehend the threat posed by cults, one must have a full understanding of what these people believe. Anyone absorbed in this subject would be wise to read the Bible as well as any of the many books that deal with Old Testament beliefs. Once one begins such studies, everything will fall into line. One of the problems today in law enforcement investigations of occult related crimes is the lack of knowledge about the occult.

Most investigators fail to realize that they are dealing with a religion that is fully covered under the First Amendment of the U.S. Constitution. In Ohio, Satanists are protected by law in offering animal sacrifices, as long as they raise the animals that they use for sacrifices. It is the same law that protects those of the the Jewish faith in preparing their kosher meats, using special methods to kill and prepare the animals.

Law enforcement officers often don't realize that Satanism is a recognized religion, its members being entitled to all the protection the First Amendment grants. It's not inconceivable that a law officer might be assigned to protect a coven's gathering. As unusual as this might sound, it really isn't far-fetched.

Those readers who may be involved in law enforcement will find that the smart investigator will keep an open and clear mind. He will try to understand what these people are doing. Some day one's life may depend upon such knowledge. The non-traditional, self-styled Satanists with self-appointed high priests are extremely dangerous. There is a distinction between different practitioners of Satanism. Just as there are many different types of mainline religions, so it is with Satanists. There are many different types and they have different ways of practicing their religion.

The varieties are many: there are homosexual covens, necrophiliac covens, cannibalism covens. It goes on and on and on. Non-traditional Satanists utilize animal sacrifices; if the opportunity arises, it's possible they will attempt human sacrifices. Non-traditional Satanists may follow the workings or the writings of the traditional Satanists to a certain point. This stands true in mainline Christian demoninations.In any study of Christianity, you will learn that at one point there was one type of religion. From that particular religion came the breaking away, came the sprouts, the shoots, until we arrive at today, with many different denominations.

This is also true in Satanism. We must always use the terms self-stylist or non-traditional and not get the traditional Satanists confused with these people. The best illustration of the traditional Satanist is Anton LaVey, who labels himself a traditionalist. He has appeared on every major television talk show. He even played the role of Satan in the 1968 motion picture, "Rosemary's Baby." LaVey is the author of *The Satanic Bible, The Satanic Rituals* and *The Complete Witch.* More than 500,000 copies of *The Satanic Bible* have been sold, admits the publisher, Avon Books.

LaVey says that Christianity once existed, but only to control the large masses of people. The "High Priest" of The Church of Satan in San Francisco, LaVey claims that true Christianity no longer exists today. He offers an "affiliation" with his church upon payment of $50.00. That money will bring the new "member" an identification card, an amulet bearing the symbol of the Church of Satan, a year's subscription to their publication called "The Cloven Hoof," and "information on how to progress more deeply into Satanism — its philosophy, rituals, locations, means of meeting other Satanists, and sources of supply for working material unique to Satanic magic." The handbill that LeVey distributes adds that new members will "receive a questionnaire, should you wish to apply for Active Membership status."

This author believes that LaVey contradicts himself by talking about Christianity no longer being in existence and yet saying his people indulge in all the deadly sins. If Christianity no longer exists, then why do his followers go against all the deadly sins that he says are mentioned in the Scriptures? I find that amusing.

There is one thing in common between traditional and non-traditional Satanists: their leaders are usually charismatic. Leaders have included such notorious figures as Charles Manson and Jim Jones. The latter, you will remember, took more than 900 followers to their deaths. Charles Manson, who led the cult that murdered actress Sharon Tate and her friends, described himself as Christ.

There are many other groups with charismatic leaders. These groups can become very dangerous. What makes them extremely dangerous is their willingness to follow the orders of their leaders or high priest.

3

Recruitment

Usually the non-traditional Satanists are fanatically secretive. It's not a simple matter for anyone interested in affiliating with a cult to go out and say, "I want to join." Becoming a Satanist is not as easy as joining a mainline denomination of a church. This just doesn't happen.

If a person is not recruited, but chooses to join a Satanic coven, the background investigation will be extremely thorough.

It is necessary to remember that Satanists are protected under the First Amendment but that Satanism itself is not recognized as truly existing in today's society. Most of the people involved in Satanism come from all walks of life. Members include physicians, attorneys, police officers, pastors, housewives, blue collar workers, teenagers, white collar workers and teenagers. The list goes on and on.

The one thing that Satanists want to protect is their identity. The fact is, they know if they are exposed as being

Satanists, or worshipping Satan, that professionally they will be finished. They know that they are protected in the worship of their religion under the First Amendment, but they are very concerned about being exposed.

This probably is why outsiders can be placed in mortal danger by attempting to put the light of publicity on any coven or by attempting to identify members of Satanic cults.

In the recruitment process by Satanists, background investigation is thorough because members want to be sure of exactly who is coming into their group. They will do all they can to guard against infiltration by an undercover agent. Informants face tremendous danger.

Informants will be found with their hearts or their tongues cut out. The latter action symbolizes that the informant has betrayed the oath of secrecy that he had sworn to. Unless the person up for membership has been a native-born member of that particular community and is well-known to other Satanist members, extra precautions are taken. When a new member is recruited, he will not be exposed to secret rituals such as animal sacrifices. New members will not be asked to eat human flesh. These rituals will be allowed only after other members are certain that the new member is sincere in his beliefs and can be trusted with the secrets of the coven.

New members won't be asked to drink human blood; they won't be asked to participate in sexual orgies; they won't be asked to become intimate with a homosexual high priest. These events will be kept secret from the new members.

Cults look for middle- to upper-class people, people who have an education and are willing to make a lifetime commitment. Where do they find such people?

Members assigned to recruiting are well trained. They look for adolescents, going to train stations, to bus stations, searching for kids with knapsacks on their backs. They'll go to counseling clinics, knowing that those people already have problems and may be searching for solutions. Recruiters will focus on Christians who have had bad experiences, such as marital problems or the loss of a child. People who are down on Christianity will be sought out. Recruiters will use the argument, "If this was a good God, why would He let such things happen to you?"

Recruiters get such discouraged persons involved. They begin to drive a wedge, to begin a separation. Newly recruited members are cut off from communication except with others within the group. Everyone becomes an enemy except those who are in the group. Everyone outside is the enemy. Police officers, Mom and Dad, friends: all are the enemy. Satanists tell prospective members that others don't understand their problems, but that Satanism provides the answers.

The Christian God, say the Satanists, is a joke. For instance, Christianity speaks against homosexuality, thus denying homosexuals the chance to practice. This causes harm, say the Satanists. A good God, they assert, would allow full reign of homosexuality. A good God would approve of bestiality. If a person wants to have sex with animals, or with the dead, the Satanists say, go ahead.

These are the tools the Satanists use, these are the stages that Satanists employ to snare their victims. Lack of sleep and lack of nutritious foods can work wonders for those seeking to recruit to their cause. Pressure is applied on the confused to impress them that the Satanists are the only ones who care, the only ones who can offer a way out.

A newly-recruited Satanist will want nothing to do with parents or spouse. They are completely isolated and committed to that particular group or high priest. Once a new member reaches a certain point, he will do anything asked by a high priest or others in the coven. Reaching that point is what is called "snapping." Once a prospect "snaps," he no longer will be in reality, no longer have control of himself, no longer have control of his own mind. The high priest, this charismatic leader, now controls the new member completely.

He controls the minds, the thought patterns. He tells the recruit what to do, when to do it and how to do it. He never gives a reason why, but new recruits will follow the commands of the high priests. This is when these new recruits become very dangerous.

If there is such a leader — a Charles Manson or those in the MOVE group in Philadelphia or the Rev. Jim Jones, a teacher who claims that all outside influences are the enemy, then there is a recipe for tragedy. I think it's very important that there be no more People's Temples, no more Jonestowns, no more Charles Manson types.

We must educate ourselves and others to recognize these people and to nip the bud before it blossoms into a destructive force. Young people who have been recruited into Satanism have told me that they have desecrated cemeteries, smashed tombstones, broken into churches, stolen things from churches, ripped up Bibles, desecrated walls in churches, dug up graves and offered bodies in sacrifice to Satan.

I must emphasize that anyone who stumbles onto such a scene could very well be killed. This is what will be done by the self-stylist, the non-traditional Satanist. In the recruitment, when the "snapping" occurs, the new member becomes totally committed to the cause and becomes dedicated to that cause. Such a person would offer anyone up into sacrifice. That person would not consider such an action true murder, but a sacrifice to his God, who is Satan.

A young woman in the MOVE group, one of two survivors in the raid by Philadelphia police, made the statement in an interview that she had no remorse for anything they had ever done. She believed that she was right and stated that she would do everything the same as she had done before.

Some people do not consider "snapping" to be a form of brainwashing, but I disagree. When it comes to this point, when the group controls the mind, then such new members have gone through a brainwashing process.

43

Satanists offer some heady prizes. Power. Position. Money. Drugs. Probably the most significant is power.

Every state has been touched. There have been thousands of animal mutilations reported across the country. Probably there have been just as many never reported to law authorities. These self-appointed high priests get their starts from the number of books offered in the average book stores. Movies are readily available in video stores. Such films as "The Exorcist," "Ghoulies," and "The Brotherhood of Satan" in themselves serve as recruiting posters, so to speak, for the Satanist movement. The ideas come from such films. In one movie, a character offers up a baby for sacrifice. This particular film has had a tremendous influence as a teaching tool.

Also important in promoting Satanism is heavy metal music that deals with death, killing and Satanism. Groups such as Motley Crue don't attempt to disguise who they are singing for. Such songs as "Children of the Beast" and "Shout at the Devil" are examples. Some of the heavy metal bands use the accouterments of Satanism in their dress, such as chains and the inverted pentagram. And such musicians promote total rebellion against authority and nearly everything else.

Another group, Venom, is especially blatant about those they are promoting. They are off the streets of Salem and they talk about killing children at night. They are totally obsessed with death.

I will discuss the influence of the heavy metal rock groups in greater detail in a later portion of this book.

A self-appointed high priest, influenced by the teachings of books, films and heavy metal groups, doesn't find much trouble in locating others who will think the same way. A charismatic leader can have a tremendous influence on young people.

Recruitment is not a simple matter of going door to door. That doesn't happen. No one is going to knock on your front door and introduce themselves as members of the Church of Satan in Hometown, U.S.A. They won't ask you to join. These people are well trained. What they do is focus on areas such as train stations, bus stations and counseling clinics, etc.

Recruiters are looking for the middle- to upper-class person who is searching for something, who is seeking a philosophy, a person who is not sure of himself, a person who wants to change the world, a person who does not believe in the democratic system and thinks he can change this country. These are the kind of people the Satanists want.

Satanism is a religion of the flesh, while Christianity is a religion of faith. To many investigators, Satanism is pure humanism. This explains its appeal to so many people. You mustn't believe that all runaways and missing children are simply gone. Some are not big enough to run away. Many investigators believe that some of these young people have been kidnapped. It is within the realm of possibility that some missing children are offered up in sacrifices. Officers have gone in on raids and have confiscated letters which clearly state that Satanism is being practiced. People have been taken from one area to another and offered as sacrifices.

Becoming fair game for the Satanists are hitchhiking youngsters and children on the streets, both male and female, working as prostitutes. These children simply vanish. There are times when such disappearances could be abductions for the purpose of sacrifices. When these abductions occur, they often are written off as being sex crimes.

It is the duty of everyone, from law enforcement officers to members of the general public, to educate themselves as to the dangers that are out there. The simple fact is that Satanism is becoming more and more blatant. Beyond the shadow of a doubt, more and more homicide cases are being reopened, because officers are taking a closer look at them as the departments become more curious about the occult. Police officers have a moral responsibility to warn people about what's happening. Whether warnings are heeded, that's

45

neither here nor there. In one case, a young girl described how she had become involved with a Satanic coven and with animal sacrifices. She said that she had made a blood pact with Satan and had willed her soul to him. She was not able to leave the coven because other members had threatened her life. As of this writing, she still is involved with that coven.

Another case involved Richard Kasso, who at age 17 was a high priest in the Knights of the Black Circle, a Satanic group in the Suffolk County, New York. He and another teenager were accused of conducting a ritualistic slaying of another 17-year-old boy. Kasso allegedly forced the victim to say, "I love Satan" before he died. Kasso stabbed the victim several times and gouged out his eyes. The slayer told authorities that "the Devil had ordered him to kill" this young man. After his arrest, Kasso fashioned bedsheets into a rope and hanged himself in his cell.

According to the *New York Times*, Kasso was a member of a group which had 20 teenage members and had held gatherings for several years in the Newport, N.Y. area involving "the sacrifice of animals, the burning and torturing of animals" in Satanic rituals.

The Kasso case was blamed on drugs, particularly the animal tranquilizer called "angel dust." Before his suicide, Kasso had told authorities that the victim had stolen from him ten bags of the powerful hallucinogen.

The mayor of the town where the horrific killing occurred told the *Times* reporter that the village of neat homes on tree-lined streets had many recreation and aid programs for young people, including a drug rehabilitation center supported by the local school district.

"We have everything a kid wants," the mayor told the newspaper.

The Kasso case, which occurred in the summer of 1984, renewed the continuing controversy over the influence of heavy metal rock groups which cultivate Satanic imagery.

When Kasso was arrested, he was wearing a shirt with the logo of AC-DC. That group boasts a Satanic image. The band's recording of "Hell's Bells" says, "Satan'll get ya!" and "You're only young, but you're gonna die!"

Police reported that at least four teenagers witnessed the slaying, in which Kasso plunged a knife 17 times into the head, neck and chest of the victim.

It can be instructive to look at some cases, so that a link can be established and it can be determined just what these people are capable of doing.

One recently reported case involved a cemetery grave that had been opened. The report read, "Persons or unknown persons tried to dig up a grave. The hole measured five feet long, three feet wide and seven feet deep. Nothing had been removed." In many instances, bones are being removed from coffins and used in ritualistic ceremonies. Also, there is a ritual that requires coffin nails. It's likely that these persons attempted to get into a grave because they assumed the coffin would be wooden and rotted, making it easy to obtain coffin nails. This is not an uncommon action among Satanists.

A very young lady who had left a Satanic group related how she had become a child of Satan in a vial blood sacrifice ceremony. She said she had helped dig up bodies from fresh graves. Those corpses then were sacrificed to Satan. This is not an unusual occurrence.

Another case reported was that a priest was upset because a Satanist removed infants from their graves and offered them to Satan. This person also was melting the body fat from the corpses and making candles. Babies' bodies are desirable because they are "pure" and therefore more power can be derived from them.

One can never charge off an open grave to a mere prankster out for a good time. While that sort of prank occurs, you can be certain that if there is cult activity in an area, grave robbing will be the work of Satanists, in most cases. They often will select an old cemetery that is seldom used and preferably isolated, where they can operate without fear of being detected.

In one case, an individual broke into a grave and cut the head from a corpse. He removed the head upon orders of a high priest. This individual kept the head in his home. When law officers went in on a raid, with a search warrant, they found the head.

Every group employs different methods. In this coven, a head bearer was used. This person was ordered by the high priest to go into a cemetery, desecrate a grave and remove the head of a corpse.

In other cases, Satanists have dug up bodies and used those bodies in various ceremonies.

If evidence of desecration is discovered in a cemetery or mausoleum, authorities should inspect the desecrated coffin to make sure that all parts of the body remain. Many times, Satanists remove bones because they believe that bones can be "read" to tell the future. Some groups, instead of utilizing a chalice to drink blood, will employ a human skull as a substitution for the chalice. In one ceremony, Satanists believe that by digging a certain depth and standing upon that coffin, they receive powers from the corpse within the coffin.

Smart investigators should make notations, take photographs and look beyond that particular area, to search for rings of rocks or of fire. Investigators should look in trees for other paraphenalia or artifacts that may be there. They should search for sticks on the ground that point in a certain direction. Officers who realize what they're seeing should treat any such area as they would in a homicide investigation. Onlookers should be kept away. Officers should search for black wax drippings on headstones around the immediate area. Black wax would be a clue as to who opened the grave. It's not every day that people burn black candles.

When a grave is disturbed in any manner, officers would

be well advised to check with someone who is well-versed in Satanism.

One young person related that he and his brother would check obituaries, selecting deceased individuals at random, then go to the funeral home to observe the bodies. The brothers would know from newspaper obituaries where the body was to be buried. The night after the funeral, while the dirt was still soft, the brothers would go to the cemetery and dig up the body. They would then remove anything that was valuable from the coffin.

They were asked how they could get through a concrete vault. "It's absolutely no problem," they responded. "We can pop those vaults like an egg shell."

One investigator discovered an unusual abandoned campsite in a wooded area. Its central feature was a ring of large stones that encircled a cow's skull mounted on a wooden stake.

Law enforcement officers found a worship site in a desolate former strip-mining area. They found a five-pointed star with stones circling it and a limestone slab in the middle, smeared with animal blood.

In another case, a cow's head was placed inside a telephone booth. The head had been mutilated in a bizarre pattern with a sharp instrument. The eyes had been carefully removed.

In yet another case, a cow was mutilated. It appeared to have just bedded down for the night in a cornfield. Its head had been removed, leaving about 18 inches of its spine protruding. To perform such a rite, it was necessary to have time and knowledge to remove the head. There was no sign of struggle and no sign of blood at the scene.

There was another case involving the skinning of rabbits alive. The animals had been removed from a cage, skinned and then placed back into the cage. There was no blood found at the scene.

There's a simple reason why blood is usually not found in such cases. Most people involved in such ritualistic ceremonies utilize that blood. They believe that the power is in the blood, that they will take on the lifeforce of the animal they kill. The only way they can do this is by drinking the blood. In most cases, they seek the maximum force of power from an animal and that's accomplished by torturing the animal. As their adrenalin peaks, they drain and drink the blood.

Autopsies on the animals are highly recommended in all investigations. Authorities who work closely with humane societies find the latter are in most cases cooperative and willing to foot the cost of the autopsies.

There are certain things the veterinarian should be asked to look for when he is completing the autopsy. He needs to check the animal for evidence of electrocution. He needs to probe the esophagus for any sign of a freon type substance there. He should check for blood remaining in the veins. Determining the time and cause of death should be noted, as well as the animal's age.

Providing such information, the veterinarian can play a tremendous role in any investigation. It's important to have autopsies done and not to depend on guesswork to figure out exactly what happened.

For example, a call was received that a small piglet had been found. This pig's sex organs and one ear were missing. From that description, it was thought it might have been used in a ritual. The left ear could have been taken as an amulet, as well as the sex organs. The deputy was advised to borrow a bag and bring the piglet to investigators so a close look could be taken. Then the carcass was sent to a veterinarian for an autopsy.

The pig had all the appearances of being used for a ritualistic sacrifice. However, there were puncture marks on the pig's back, and the possibility arose of it being an animal kill, and not a Satanic-type sacrifice. The autopsy showed that the pig had died of pneumonia and apparently had been discarded in a field by its owner. The veterinarian decided that the missing ear and sex organs, as well as the back punctures were caused by a dog. The puncture marks resulted when the dog carried the pig in its mouth and then deposited the dead animal on a resident's front lawn.

Veteran investigators of the occult and Satanic groups should guard against sensationalism and overdramatizing such finds until it's clear what has happened. Officers shouldn't speak to the press unless they're certain of information. It might have been easy to have described this find as the result of a ritualistic ceremony. Officers must protect their credibility; it's extremely important.

Police authorities quickly learn that it's easy to give the news media what they want. It's easy to be on the news every night and in the papers. For investigators, it's more important to check with the professionals, sift through evidence and utilize all the tools available to make certain that finds are cult-related. I urge authorities not to make a report until the investigation is complete. And I urge them to stress that the report is their personal opinion, that the report is not necessarily the final word.

In another case, a pentagram and circle were discovered in an abandoned house. In the middle of the circle was an animal that appeared to have been sacrificed in a Satanic ritual. When the investigators first looked at that particular photograph, the pentagram looked too perfect. There are such places that have pentgrams that are painted and are done with exact measurements, and in extensive detail, but in my most personal dealings with non-traditional Satanists, I've found them to be sloppy people who make sloppy pentagrams. Pentagrams usually are drawn on the ground or painted on a building very crudely.

In this particular abandoned house, however, the pentagram was carefully worked out. The case got tremendous publicity. But it came out later that everything was a hoax. The dead animal had been struck by a car and then been placed inside the circle as a joke. It's common for publicity hounds to attempt to fool investigators.

In one case I investigated, the second floor of an abandoned house contained a circle with the pentagram inside, painted in red. In making measurements, it was observed that the pentagram was weathered. It obviously had been there a long period of time. On the windows, black plastic had been installed to keep out light and to prevent candlelight used in ceremonies from reaching the outside. But the plastic was torn and weatherbeaten. It hadn't been placed there recently.

On the third floor, in an attic area, a spot had been cleared. A ladder apparently had been moved from the barn into the house to make it possible to reach the attic from the second floor. It was apparent that services had been held in that attic. There was an animal carcass in the attic and another in the basement.

But in the official report, I could not say that these animals had been sacrificed. It was possible that they could have crawled into the house and died. It would have been easy for me to report that these animals were the victims of a Satanic cult. But I could not prove it.

However, there was an authentic pentagram on the second floor, and I had no doubts about its authenticity. This is the sort of thing investigators should look for.

When a pentagram is found, also check to see if it is weathered. Determining its age can be helpful. Always take photos, which will be invaluable as time passes. Try to determine the direction of the pentagram, how it's pointed.

In this case, a human-like doll was discovered. This was the second site in that county in which a doll had been found. It appeared that the dolls had been used in a Satanic ritual along with sympathetic-type magic. One doll had been burned; the breasts' nipples were scorched. The doll had been slit open. It seemed logical that the doll had been used symbolically to represent a living person and that Satanists had been having ceremonies, practicing black magic and seeking harm to come to the person that the doll was intended to represent.

As has been stated earlier, an investigator doesn't have to be a believer in Satanism. But investigators must never forget that Satanists believe fervently in what they are doing. Investigators are dealing in spiritual warfare. Many hours may be spent in investigations, with few tangible results. There will be frustration, as one works for many, many hours. There probably won't be sufficient information to lead to an arrest; investigators will find it terribly difficult to uncover sufficient information to file charges. Talking to such investigators across the nation produces similar stories. The battle is tough and never ending.

Authorities will be dealing with secrecy and with very small groups of people. It's easy for members to travel in vans, to move services around, to use isolated areas, roads not heavily traveled, old, unused cemeteries, abandoned barns, old and unused churches, isolated fields, heavily wooded areas, or even riverbanks.

A young man fishing under a bridge called me. He said he had been there all night. In the early morning, he heard chanting. He walked over to see what was happening. He witnessed robed figures in a circle, around a fire, chanting. He did not realize that he was placing himself in mortal danger.

The Satanists saw him and they pursued him. He got away and called. I'm convinced he told the truth. He described the people. He said they were traveling in a pickup truck.

Authorities will not be dealing with people riding buses, with caravans going into an area. Authorities deal with a very small group of people that knows exactly what it is doing. And such groups do not intend to be interrupted during services. Members of covens will leave animals behind as personal calling cards, to let others know that they are practicing in the area.

I tell investigators that they shouldn't worry about making arrests, or getting their name on marquee lights. I urge them to focus on education, on the investigation, on the possibility of exposing these people, letting them know that law officers know who they are, and that law enforcement officers know what they are doing. But I caution investigators to guard against infringing on their First Amendment right. Don't trip up, I tell those attending my seminars. Trampling on the rights of Satanists can cause all sorts of legal problems.

I always tell my seminar groups to never approach a ritual in progress alone. A single law officer would be in mortal danger. One might get in, but Satanists would never allow that person to get out.

One report described teenagers initiated into a coven in which they ate entrails while the animal's heart still was beating. It also described sacrificing dogs, their blood being consumed at worship services. *The Los Angeles Herald Examiner* said that a young inmate at the Santa Cruz County Jail told of the initiation.

There now are acid cults, which rely heavily on drugs to entice members and to keep them. *The San Francisco Chronicle* reported that a group of Satan worshippers tortured and beat a 17-year-old youth to death. He was tied to a bed and whipped, then moved to a basement altar room. The room had a long black table on which candles had been placed, along with blackened bottles. The young man was flogged with chains and slashed with broken bottles. He was found in a wooded area. His head had been crushed.

More and more of these reports are coming in.

Nudity is becoming a common element in Satanic covens. When a woman is initiated, she is symbolically sacrificed. In the ceremony, she lies naked on the altar. She is nude because of the Satanists belief that clothes restrict their power.

The priest then will have sexual intercourse with the initiate; then other male members of the coven also will have sex with the woman.

Anton LaVey, high priest in San Francisco, says that sex between consenting adults is nobody's business. All Satanists who have read *The Satanic Bible* are familiar with LaVey's views on homosexuality. Satanism condones any type of sexual activity which properly satisfies an individual's desires, be it homosexuality, bisexuality, even asexuality if the Satanist so prefers. Satanism also sanctions any fetish or deviation which will enhance a member's sex life.

I was asked by a person during an investigation if when people get involved they find they can't handle such sexual perversion mentally, do they ever go off the deep end. The answer is, of course, yes.

A young woman, ten days before her death, spoke to a reporter. She told him how deeply troubled and involved she was with Devil worship. She described how she was afraid of the Devil cult. She said she couldn't go on any longer, after she watched a privately-made film that showed an actual human sacrifice. She was forced to view a "snuff film" and she committed suicide.

A young man, was arrested for speeding. He said he was being chased by a Devil cult after he attended a black magic party. He said the group was holding fertility rites and that he refused to drink the blood of a freshly killed dog. He fled. After that time, he said the group persecuted him. "I don't want to say anything about the cult, because I will die if I do," he told authorities.

4

Overview

Paganism began thousands of years ago when people generally stopped their roaming, settled down and began an agrarian existence. New problems arose, however, in man's effort to survive. Paganism has been called man's first attempt at technology, his initial effort to obtain control of his environment.

Paganists selected certain people to be in charge of these efforts toward technology. Shamans, Witch doctors and medicine men often were chosen because of unique characteristics. These leaders often suffered from such things as epilepsy, blindness or albinism. Shamans gave human characteristics to natural things. They gave natural forces human names. After choosing a name for an environmental unit, the Shaman would then attempt to communicate with it, by various means. Often such attempts at communication failed, or were subject to interpretation made by the Shaman, who of course gave the most personally advantageous definition to his efforts. When a Shaman's efforts proved in vain, the wise one would tell his followers that the "gods" required or demanded gifts or sacrifices. Many contemporary tribal cultures continue to practice this type of religion and communication with natural spirits and forces. Observances and rituals utilized in present-day religions include out-of-body travel, spirit guides in the forms of animals (familiars), ritual gifts and sacrifices.

Confusion resulted during the middle ages when Christianity and paganism collided. There was a blending of Christian and pagan beliefs as compromise was used to keep peace and encourage societal acceptance.

Many pagan traditions continue in force today. Modern American society can easily identify religion and philosophy that dates to ancient Greek, Roman and Egyptian worship and beliefs. There is a difference between natural religions and those religions which derive from some type of "divine revelation."

Paganism centers around goddess worship or the worship of the "earth mother" or the "huntress." Symbol of the goddess is the moon, in most cases. The most common form of goddess worship is wiccan, which is a masculine noun. The feminine form of this word is wicce and the performance of wicce beliefs is called wicce-craft or witchcraft. Various forms of the wiccan religion include Gardnerian magic, Crowlish magic, Druidism and Neodruidism, and Shamanism. Throughout history, persons practicing the wiccan religions have been stigmatized, ostracized, persecuted and murdered. As we all are aware from our history classes in school, many persons have been accused and convicted on practicing witchcraft, even though their actual involvement was miniscule or totally absent. In other cases, true witches managed to escape notice by effectively blending into society.

(For interviews that I conducted with four practicing pagans, turn to Chapter Thirteen.)

There often has been confusion between true paganism and the concept depicted in countless Hollywood motion pictures. Paganism often includes "circle magic," where the goddess or some other force is summoned by the witch. The purpose of pagan rituals is to summon positive or negative forces at a time when the doors between the world of the living and the dead aren't normally open. Pagans are convinced that these doors to that strange "other world" are thrust wide on April 30th and October 31st every year. But pagans also believe that if the doors are not open, they can be forced through the use of ritual magic.

Many of the ceremonies practiced by pagans resemble those carried out by Satanists. Hallmarks of the pagan ritual ceremony includes a circle large enough to contain the worshipping group and artifacts used in the ritual. Generally found inside the ritual circle is an altar, which has been consecrated. Altars are never left behind after a ceremony ends. The keeper of the ritual is required to protect the altar and make sure that it is secured after the ceremony. Persons attending such ceremonies often wear different colored robes with flowing hoods. Others will be "sky clad," which means that they are completely naked. The chalice used in the ceremony represents the female sexual organ; the athame — usually at least nine inches long — represents the male sexual organ.

The protective sealing of the ritual areas is absolutely vital to the safety of the participants from the attacks of negative forces which may come forth. Pagans believe that an accidental or unintentional break in the ritual circle will allow the howling hoards of hell to enter the ritual area uncontrolled. In order to be safe, successful and effective, rituals must be flawlessly performed.

Homosexuals often are comfortable with paganism, since it involves the worship of a goddess-mother figure. It has been reported that homosexuals often work in witchcraft stores, where they can learn magic and also make homosexual contacts in the process.

Confusion often occurs in discussion of the various forms of magic. Pagans make a distinction between "negative force" and "positive force." Black magic is used for bad purposes, such as summoning up negative forces to perform evil works. White magic is employed to do good. It has been pointed out that all magic stems from the same source, regardless of the alleged object of the magical rite. In the pagan tradition, any group (often called a coven) can perform either black or white magic, depending upon the purposes or objects desired. (The pagans I interviewed for the material used in Chapter Thirteen vigorously deny that they practice any kind of black magic and claim to shun any person who does delve into the black arts.)

Paganism uses many types of talismans or symbols believed to possess magical traits. Talismans are thought to be devices of power, sacred objects and active symbols. Amulets are worn to protect the wearer. Besides the inverted pentagram, which represents Satan, other symbols include representations of specific goddesses, deities, or spirits as well as astrological signs. Alphabets of ancient writings are often used in incantations and communications.

There are many offshoots and different traditions which employ the same basic philosophies as paganism.

Those who have closely followed the recent outbreaks of Satan worship nationwide have observed that much of this so-called worship by teenagers combines elements of paganism, Satanism, Hollywood hype and the influence of these persons' personal lusts and desires. Fantasy role-playing games such as Dungeons & Dragons fit into the pagan philosophy in that such games allow individuals to act out personal fantasies for mastery and control over others. I'll get more deeply into the problem of fantasy games in a later section of this book.

Several publishers sell books to anyone which explain in

detail methods of assassination used by the Thugees, the Ninja and the Society of Assassins. Although these books are purportedly offered as augmentation to fantasy role-playing games, they offer explicit details on which weapons can be used to kill others. These books give instructions on making poisons and other agents of death "from scratch." The books are sold through game, book and hobby stores.

SATANISM

Moving from paganism to Satanism, it must be noted that Satanism usually does not involve the intense ritualization that can be seen in pure paganism. Satanists often don't bother to construct ritual circles to ward off demons. Why? Because they simply don't care. Their intention is to bring about close intercourse with Satan and his demons.

Police authorities have agreed that today Satanism can be broken up into three basic groupings: (1) adult groups, (2) adult and adolescent groups, and (3) adolescent groups. Law enforcement officials believe that the second group combining adults and adolescents brings about the most extreme potential for abuse and death of children if those children aren't related to the adults in the group.

The all-adolescent groups usually are experimenters with Satanic rituals. They seldom are sincere, involved or knowledgeable practitioners of pure traditions. Officials point out that the fact that these youngsters' ignorance of the implications and ritualized skills by no means infers that adolescent Satanism is less dangerous than that practiced by other groups. Involvement usually brings addiction, which leads to deeper involvement. Some authorities have estimated that at least a third of those involved in totally adolescent groups have the potential to kill.

A seminar held in Jacksonville, Florida, during 1986 made

the point that pure Satanism requires intense training, initiation, screening, rituals and rites and an upward mobility within the Satanic worship structure. Pure Satanism is seen worldwide and (as with other deviant movements) is well-established in many forms, is multi-national, and has almost inexhaustible financial and physical resources.

Satanic rituals have some parallels with pagan rituals. Satanists also find a site which is isolated to insure privacy, Each Satanic group has its own gremoire, also called "The Book of Shadows." The Book of Shadows is used to write rituals, incantations and names. This book can be important evidence about the depth, structure and activities of any particular Satanic group.

ORDO TEMPLI ORIENTIS

Much of today's Satanism is based to some extent on the teachings of Aleister Crowley, who belonged to a group called Ordo Templi Orientis at the turn of the century.

Crowley was born in Leamington, Warwickshire, England in 1875 to Quaker parents. Crowley was reared in a group called the Plymouth Brethren. He entered the Order of the Golden Dawn in 1898. He gained a reputation over the next two decades for breaking every moral law on the books, from fornication to murder. In 1904 Crowley claimed that he received a communication from the "astral" with instructions for establishing a "new order," which he set up in 1907. Crowley joined Ordo Templi Orientis and was made the head of its British affiliate. Crowley wrote numerous books on the occult and his teachings have become the bylaws of modern Satanism.

Crowley's teachings can be summed up by quoting some of his more infamous statements. He taught that "Good is evil and evil is good." His tenet, "Do what thou wilt shall be the whole of the law" is currently used on Ordo Templi Orientis literature which seeks new members. Crowley also wrote, "Thou has no right but to do thy will. Do that, and no other shall say nay." He also said that "man has the right to live by his own will, eat what he will, think what he will, love as he will. Man has the right to kill those who would thwart these rights. Love is the law, love under will."

Crowley's so-called commandments have been adopted by occultists, who believe Crowley's teachings give them the liberty to murder, mutilate and cannibalize anyone or eat anything.

According to a report issued by a police department in California, a later leader of OTO, Jack Parsons, took L. Ron Hubbard into the OTO. Hubbard was reported never to have formally joined the organization. The two men parted ways in 1946 and later Hubbard denied any attachment to OTO. Hubbard, now dead, became famous as founder of the Church of Scientology as well as being the author of many science fiction novels.

The group continues in existence today and appears to be particularly active in California. Police reports show that OTO groups have been uncovered in Berkeley, California, as well as in Stockton, California. The OTO unit in the latter city distributes a handbill which defines Ordo Templi Orientis as "a magicko-mystical fraternity that furthers the precepts set forth by the great masters: Lao Tzu, Shiddhartha, Krishna, Mosheh (Moses), Dionysus, Mahmud (Mohammed), and the master Therion (Aleister Crowley).

"The OTO has existed in one form or another throughout the ages, and can lay claim to a direct descendence from the Knights Templar. The OTO is an international religious body with an encampment now in Stockton." The handbill concludes that the group welcomes all inquiries.

One reasonable estimate of cults, sects and deviant movements in existence today in the U.S. puts their number at between 500 and 600. Those are just the ones that are currently active. The potential numbers reach the 2,000 mark, according to knowledgeable sources.

The United States has seen a tremendous rise in cult and sect activities in the past quarter-century. Some experts claim that as many as 25 million Americans are directly affected by cult and sect influence. History has shown that dealings with such groups has been extremely difficult for the law enforcement community as well as the military. Of course, one principal reason is that such cults and sects are able to utilize the protection granted by the Constitution to freedom of religion. The courts have traditionally had a difficult time in deciding which are legitimate religions and which are groups that exist only to prey upon their members or upon society itself. Thus it becomes relatively easy for cults and sects to flourish, since the law offers the same amount of protection to them as it does to more mainstream, more legitimate organizations.

Many such offbeat, quasi-religious groups employ well-trained, highly disciplined and organized agents who work to infiltrate the police and the military. Often well-financed, these groups are hardly fly-by-night operations.

The majority of religious and political movements have a charismatic figure as leader. Such a leader often claims an extraordinary and divine experience which sets him apart from others. Or he will assert some type of special political ideology that is unique to the time and area in which it emerges. Those claiming divine guidance usually are at the head of a religious cult, while those who say they possess special political ideology will most often head political movements. Sometimes, however, the political and religious lines become intertwined, resulting in what has been labeled identity church movements.

A deviant group usually can mark its greatest success in recruiting new members (as mentioned in an earlier chapter) when those potential recruits are undergoing great stress or change in their own lives. For example, a freshman just entering college or a new soldier in the military might be prime candidates for the clever recruiters of cults or sects. Such young people are under great stress and find themselves isolated in strange surroundings stripped of their normal peer and group support.

Others who might be candidates for the cult/sect recruiters would be adults who have just undergone stressful situations in their lives, such as farmers who have lost the fight to save their property or couples who have been battered by the pressures that erupt in failing marriages and the trauma of divorce.

If a deviant group manages to take precedence in a person's life during such a devastating period, that group may capture the person's loyalty, thought patterns and behaviors for the remainder of that person's life. By the same token, the involvement with such a group might decrease if other factors in the affected person's life reach a more stable level. The level of one's mental stability in such periods of high stress can greatly influence the chances of falling under the spell of such sects or cults.

Cults should be distinguished from other groups such as sects and religions. A cult is usually a small starting place for a deviant movement. The cult may change into a sect as its philosophy gains momentum and adherents. Society becomes more accustomed to the cult and it can then evolve into a sect, which shows more stability and acceptance. The sect then may grow and gain in acceptance until eventually it will become recognized as a religion. The entire process usually requires the passage of a number of years. For instance, the Church of Jesus Christ of Latter Day Saints, better known as the Mormons, was for many years considered a cult. As time passed, its growth and leadership made the progression to a sect and finally to a religion, one that has won the approval of a majority of the nation. One poll shows that 80 percent of those questioned now recognize Mormonism as a religion.

Cults generally have the following characteristics:

— Membership is voluntary and achieved, through some sort of test.

— A self-elitist image. Cult members often develop an "us versus them" mentality.

— Exclusivism. Members think they are the only ones possessing the truth and the only ones who will be "saved" in the event of a catastrophe.

— Hostility. Since cult members believe only they possess the truth, gradually hostility is generated against society in general. This also works in reverse, with society prejudiced against the cult because of lack of knowledge or falsehoods about the organization.

— Acetism. Cults often demand sacrfices of self-comfort, finances, etc, from their members in order to promote the group's cause. Cults often generate large sums by convincing members to turn over their personal wealth for the good of the common cause.

— Priesthood of all believers, though usually on a scale or various levels. Members often feel free to make adjustments or to take actions as long as the end justifies the means. This can lead to extremism and terrorism.

— Increasing control mechanisms. As a member goes deeper into involvement with a cult, control mechanism attack that member's independent thought and freedom of action. Such brainwashing or mind control actions include food and/or sleep deprivation, separation from one's family or peer group, as well as intense indoctrination that forbids questioning.

— Forbidding critical recourse. Members of deviant groups rarely have the opportunity to question the actions taken by the charismatic leader. If open criticism occurs, it often can lead to painful sanctions or even death for the critic.

Many such cults and/or sects are spread across the world and deal in millions of dollars. One report shows that the Unification Church, run by the Rev. Sun Myung Moon, grosses between $1 million to $1.5 million every day. The money pours in through street sales and begging by its "Moonie" members.

Another group, The Way International — its headquarters are in New Knoxville, Ohio — generates revenue from the gifts and donations of its members. Additional funds come from charging fees for training courses and through selling souvenirs and printed material. The Way even issues savings bonds in the name of the organization. The headquarters building of The Way International is valued at more than $5 million. This organization also has extensive holdings in property and equipment.

Two basic structures are found in most cults and sects. First there is the authoritarian model, in which most of the direction comes from the top, from the charismatic leader. Policies and principles of the organization are decided by its leader, and others down the line are bound to carry out those policies. Then there is the non-authoritarian model, in which those in the lower echelons of the organization have some say-so in creating or carrying out policies. It might be said that there is a smidgen of "democracy" in such groups.

One example of an authoritarian group would be The Way International. With some 150,000 members internationally, it seeks to establish a "theocracy" as an alternative to our present democratic system of government. Some authorities believe that The Way International hopes to achieve its goals by creating an army of 3.5 million persons by 1995. To many law enforcement officials, The Way International is the most aggressive and successful cult group in the U.S. today. Some say that it embodies the greatest danger for our present system of government.

Another authoritarian group would be the Unification Church, whose members believe that the Rev. Sun Myung Moon is Christ personified. Moon's aims, though combining religious and political goals, seem to be primarily political in nature. Among his goals, students of the movement claim, is taking over the government of the United States as well as enhancing and supporting the government of the Republic of Korea. The Unification Church is a prime user of mind-control techniques upon its adherents.

Non-authoritarian groups would include the Church of Scientology, the group created by the late L. Ron Hubbard. He first came to attention in the 1930s as the writer of outlandish science fiction stories and novels that were usually labeled "space operas." His book, *"Dianetics,"* is a volume that more or less sets down the basic beliefs of Scientology. It has been a best-seller for decades and is annually updated and revised. Scientology groups are active throughout the U.S. and Great Britain, generally targeting persons not less than 25 years of age. The church uses intensive psychological stripping techniques by way of "auditors" using lie detector machines. Once adherents have attained a "clear" (free from sin) status, they believe themselves to be "gods" who then can participate in the co-creation of the world. This godhood status often brings them into conflict with normal societal institutions, such as the police. The Church of Scientology expends much effort infiltrating the law enforcement community and in gaining access to police files, often using the Freedom of Information Act to achieve its aims.

The Ananda Marga is a group which started in India in the 1960s. Its members believe that only they are qualified to exercise effective control of the world. They believe that they belong in control of the universe and that they should be the only ones in charge of nuclear weapons. They hope to take nuclear weapons away from those who now control them. There is a major training center for the Ananda Marga in Steamboat Springs, Colorado.

Members of cults, surveys have shown, are overwhelmingly those who have dependent personalities. One survey estimated that at least 80 percent of the membership of such groups could be identified thusly. Many groups, in their recruitment efforts, target persons aged 18 to 26. Those within this age range often have not fully matured and have not fully worked out values or systems. Many are eager to try new things, to experience new thrills. Thus such persons can be easy marks for those who are seeking new recruits for the cult.

In the main, dependent personalities can be identified through the following indicators: intelligence, low self-esteem, low achievement, the feeling of being not lovable, feelings of isolation, problems dealing with stress and problems in social and sexual interaction.

A young person with these traits, whether they are long-standing or merely temporary because of some current stressful situation, can be called as having a "classic addict mentality."

Of course there are hundreds of other movements across the U.S. Many groups do not fall within either authoritarian or non-authoritarian guidelines, but a common characteristic is that any adherent with sufficient charisma can form his own splinter group should he decide to differ with the cult or sect.

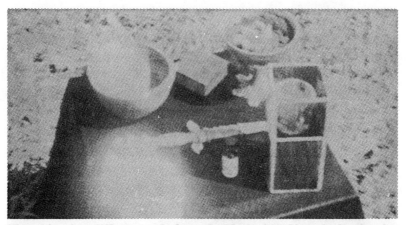

The white altar differs greatly from the black altar. Note the bowls, also the athame as well as the incense burner. The small bottle contains oil to dress down the candles that will be used in their ritual. It could be a straight candle or a figure candle depending on the ritual.

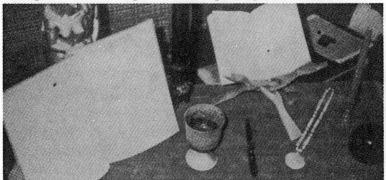

The black altar is one easily recognized. In most cases you will find incense burning with some type of mixture depending on the ritual. The mixture is used in summoning the demonic forces. Also found on the altar will be a wand, sword that is used to cast the circle, and an athame which normally is surgical steel and razor sharp, used in the sacrifice or mutilation of the animal or human. The Book of Shadows is also kept on the altar, and candles of different colors depending on the ritual. A silver chalice will also be placed on the altar. This is used to drink blood, wine or any liquid that the practitioner chooses to drink. It is not uncommon to find a bell, which is used to purify the air at the beginning of the ritual and to dismiss the evil spirits at the end of the ritual. Altars can be made from wood, limestone, marble tombstone, or a human female.

The Baphomet, sometimes called the Goat of Mendes, represents good and evil. It also represents male, female and animal. The goat head alone is the universal symbol of Satan.

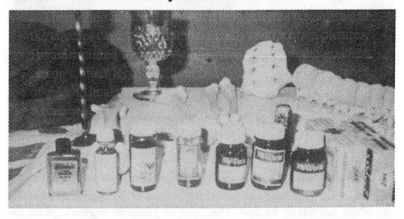

When practitioners use candles for rituals, they must dress the candle down with whatever type of oil the ritual calls for. This oil is purchased from occult shops and it can range from black arts oil to bats blood oil, depending on the ritual. These practitioners are very serious about their rituals and never take them lightly.

This is a Satanic altar. Note the human skull with black candle, chalice, figure candle, straight candle, also the top of a human skull used also as a chalice. The altar cloth is the inverted pentagram or goat's head inside the circle.

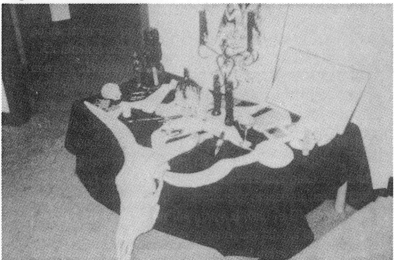

This is just a small amount of Satanic paraphernalia Tom Wedge puts on display at his seminars. Note the human skull, candles made from animal fat, which the Satanist believes has great power, next only to the fat of a baby melted down and mixed with wax to make candles.

When an inverted pentagram is found don't overlook the signs as well as the symbols that are drawn or painted inside the circle. These signs and symbols can tell you what type of ritual was used in many cases. Always photograph the pentagrams and diagrams in which directions they are pointing.

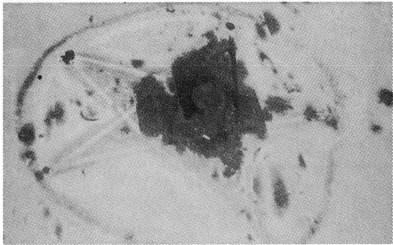

The inverted pentagram that you will find most of the time is of this type. They are very crude and quickly done. The sacrifice is made within the circle. In most cases, but not all, the sacrifice is left. Also the circle is drawn in the same manner, very crude and quickly.

Some Satanists choose abandoned buildings such as this one. They believe that evil spirits dwell in such buildings and they are power spots. The ultimate power spot is an abandoned church in an out-of-the-way location. I have spoken to Satanists who choose such places to hold rituals.

Tom Wedge holding a doll that was found at this Satanic ritual sight. The doll was used in sympathetic magic which means that this doll represents the person who has offended a member of the group or coven. This doll was the second case in the same county involving a doll being sacrificed. The other ritual sight also included an animal sacrifice as well.

Grave desecration is very common among the non-traditional Satanists. They will open graves to remove human skulls because they believe this is the power center. The Satanist will remove other bones as well. They use them to tell the future.

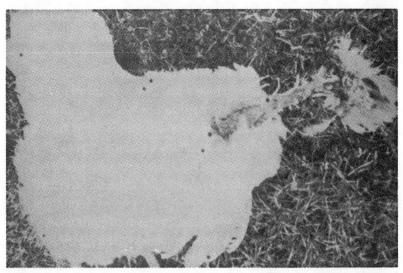

This chicken had its windpipe removed and less than a teaspoon of blood was found in its veins. Satanists will offer any type of animal, wild or domestic.

This adult cow had been used in a Satanic ritual. Its head was surgically removed from the spinal column. There was no sign of blood at the scene. In a cemetery in the same county Satanists had held initiation ceremonies where Tom found Holy Bibles that had been burned which lead him to believe this was an initiation ceremony where the neophyte pledged his allegiance to Satan and denounced Jesus Christ as the Son of God.

These lambs were sacrificed and then dumped. All of the internal organs had been removed as well as the sex organs. All of the blood had been removed.

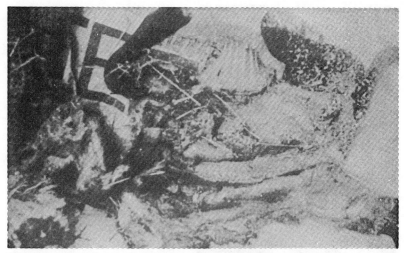

This lamb had been offered in a sacrifice to Satan. No blood was found in the lamb and all organs had been removed, including the sex organs.

This dog had been skinned and its sex organs had been removed. It was reported that the blood had been removed. The dog was left at a crossroad. This is just one of the many cases that Tom has been involved with which deals with animal mutilations.

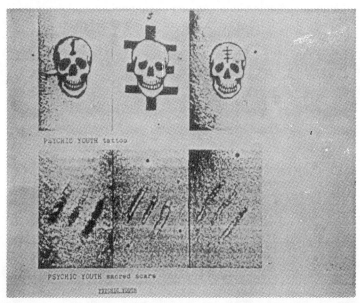

The psychic youth tattoo will appear on the upper right arm, consisting of a human skull which may or may not be dressed up. The scars are cut or burnt into the arm. Parents and law enforcement officers should remember these symbols so they can detect any early signs of those involved in this sect.

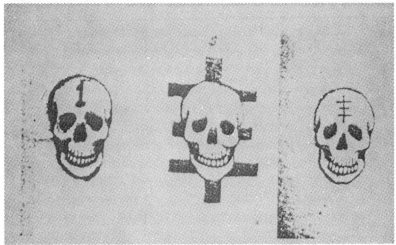

Ths skull tattoo is used by the psychic youth temple. Note: Each skull can be dressed up in any way they feel they want to dress it.

5

Black Mass

The Satanic Age was born in 1966. That's when God was proclaimed dead and so called "sexual freedom" basically began. Satanism, as always, existed prior to that point, but it then began to play a more important role.

One of the major parts of Satanism is the Black Mass. It has been described in many ways. Today, probably the most common type of practice would be described as follows:

One person within a coven is designated to go out and steal a host from a Catholic church. Another may be asked to steal holy water from a church. The Black Mass itself is a blasphemy of Christianity. The Black Mass twists the Catholic mass. The host which is blessed by the priest is believed to become the flesh of Christ; the wine that is blessed by the priest represents the blood of Christ. The point is, by stealing the host, the Satanists desecrate the Flesh of Christ. And when they steal holy water blessed by a priest and the wine, they are attacking the sacraments of the church.

The wine is defiled by urinating into it. Blood furnished by the Satanic high priest often is mixed with the urine-fouled wine. The altar used in the Black Mass is mounted by a naked female. The stolen host can then be desecrated either by urinating on it, or by inserting it into the vagina of the nude woman. Sometimes the host is used to write, in Hebrew, blasphemies against God and the church. In some instances, the host is stamped with a representation of the face of Satan, then thrown to the ground. The chalice containing the holy water or wine is placed between the woman's breasts. At this point the chalice is passed around to the members of the coven, who drink this blending of holy water, wine and urine in communion to Satan. The host is passed to the members and eaten, also in communion to the Devil. At the same time, the Lord's Prayer is read aloud, backwards.

It is an evil ceremony. Black masses are not held every week; some Satanists have told me that masses are held as little as four times annually. Others say they are held slightly more often.

The Black Mass is the ultimate ritual honoring Satan, used to blaspheme all Christianity.

RITUALS

Satanists will hold rituals in their homes, just as convicted triple murderer Sean Sellers did. The altar itself doesn't have to be elaborate. Some have been found in closets. A corner of a room can be used for this purpose.

Sellers, whose story I related in the opening pages of this book, had everything deemed necessary by Satanic groups to practice the Black Arts. He possessed chalices, though they were silver, not gold. He kept several ceremonial swords on the altar. He had the knife or the athame, a knife used in offering sacrifices. He kept a supply of candles, candleholders, and incense.

The black mass is the most diabolic, most evil of all rituals performed by some of those involved in Satanism. History shows the roots of the black mass in the 14th Century and carried through to the 15th Century. During this period, the black mass began to be performed to pay homage to Satan.

During the late 1500s, those who failed to follow the ways of the Roman Catholic church and accept it as the only true religion became disgusted. They wanted to desecrate anything and everything that stood for the church. Wine representing the blood of Jesus Christ and bread representing His flesh were the substances used in Holy Communion. Satanists replaced the host (bread) with the black turnip, human feces or sausage slices. Sometimes the host was stolen, resulting in the ultimate blasphemy. Satanists replaced the wine used in Communion with human urine, black water or some other kind of brew. Many times these ceremonies were performed by defrocked or rogue priests who were dissatisfied with the church.

The black mass was performed with a nude female lying atop the altar, which in most cases is a flat limestone or stone which has been consecrated. A nude woman was selected for the altar since at the time the black mass was devised, a woman was seen as being unclean. Women were considered such because the first woman, Eve, had been deceived by Satan in the Garden of Eden.

When Eve consumed the forbidden fruit, that action caused her banishment, along with Adam, from the Garden. Thus, according to the book of Genesis, commenced the fall of man. In the eyes of early followers of Satan, it was a true blasphemy to use a naked woman on the consecrated altar.

The rite of the black masses in the 16th century as conducted by Abbe Guibourg in Paris involved the same elements of crime and blasphemy as we see in today's world: infants being kidnapped and sold, white slavery, grave robbery, the buying and selling of fetuses along with aborted babies.

It was reported that one black mass involved the Queen of France, Catherine de Medici, whose son Phillip was slowly dying from an unknown illness. She was reputed to have commissioned a black mass. Allegedly this mass was to have called for the sacrifice of a young child and was to be performed by a defrocked priest. By seeking such a ritual, the queen was asking Satan to exchange the health of her son for the sacrifice of the young child.

In a dimly lit chamber the young child was given holy communion by the priest, thus making the child pure or sin-free. The child then was killed, his blood taken to fill the chalice. According to the writings of Ericson, Catherine de Medici wore around her neck a talisman containing the name of a demon known as Asmodeus. This demon's name is employed to this day for Satanic rituals, including one murder case that I am working on as this book is being written. This dreaded demonic force is one of the princes of Hell who is summoned to destroy and kill.

One of the most infamous characters connected with the black mass is Guibourg. By request of Louis XIV's mistress, Marquise de Montespan, a private chapel was constructed in the home of Catherine Deshayes, who was also known as La Voisin. After being tortured, La Voisin claimed that she had disposed of the bodies of more than 2,500 infants who had been used in rituals and black masses.

In 1678 de Montespan arrived at La Voisin's home and was taken to the Satanic chapel. The hideous Guibourg, then in his 60s, was called in to perform the black mass. De Montespan took off her clothes and placed her nude body on the altar, her legs spread wide and dangled over the side. Guibourg stood between de Montespan's legs and placed a chalice on her belly. He then took a consecrated host and inserted it into her vagina opening, saying, "This is my body."

Guidourg did not infer that the host was the body of Christ, but rather that it was Guibourg's body. Then Guibourg penetrated the woman.

During the next part of the ritual, two princes of Hell— Astaroth and Asmodeus — were summoned, with Guibourg offering this incantation: "Astaroth, Asmodeus, princes of friendship and of love, we invoke you to accept the sacrifice of this child which we offer to you now, that we may receive those things for which we ask."

Guibourg then held aloft an infant by its tiny feet, cut the baby's throat and let the infant's blood drain into the chalice resting on de Montespan's nude body. This offering was not that of a life for a life, but rather it was a sacrifice to call upon demonic forces to help carry out de Montespan's wishes.

At this point Guibourg removed the chalice, then completed the black mass by having sexual intercourse with the woman. When they both reached a sexual climax, Guibourg sprinkled blood from the slain baby on his own sex organs as well as those of de Montespan. At the end of the ritual, La Voisin took the consecrated host as well as the child's blood, giving them to de Montespan to mix into the king's food. She hoped that she would win the king's favors, overcoming the other mistresses that he had. The king, however, discovered the plot and de Montespan was banished from the palace.

The actions of Abbe Guibourg and La Voisin clearly show the lengths to which the twisted minds of the followers of Satan will go to achieve their demented desires.

During the 19th century much of the same types of incidents occurred. Those who practiced the Satanic rituals were men and women who had fallen away from the faith. These people are called apostates. During this period, self-proclaimed high priests would hold rituals as well as black masses.

Many of the structures used today for black masses are not as elaborate as the La Voisin chapel. Today's Satanists prefer to perform the black mass in abandoned churches, which they believe to be power spots that demonic forces will want to inhabit.

The black mass also can take place in an individual's home. Two cases that I helped to investigate involved human sacrifices or ritual murders that took place in the home. The black mass also can take place in an isolated cemetery or any appropriate place.

When the black mass is performed, it follows the general structure and verbal form of the Roman Catholic mass. But the black mass always consists of acts of blasphemy and perversion, culminating with animal or human sacrifice, followed by a sexual orgy.

The black mass is not limited to the rich or famous or to middle-class America, but is practiced by those from all walks of life, from adolescents to adults.

Satanism has spread across the U.S. It is in all states. None have gone untouched. Satanists are involved in trafficking in drugs, kidnapping, abortion, the selling of children, grave robbing and white slavery. One Satanist told me during an interview how he had stolen furniture from a church. It has been proved that semen, blood and menstrual blood have been used in today's Satanic rituals. Fat from stillborn babies or young children or aborted children is being mixed with wax for the purpose of making ritual candles and oils for dressing candles.

Those involved in the black arts sometimes use blood and semen for making potions for love or death rituals. The term vinum sabbatt identifies the liquid blood, animal or human. When someone such as myself investigates scenes involving sacrifices, either animal or human, it never appears that those victims died willingly.

Satanism today seems to go hand-in-hand with drug usage. In both capital crimes that I have been involved in, Satanism was tied in with heavy use of drugs.

Today's Satanists are more blatant than those who secretly

83

practiced their nefarious rituals in past centuries. Today's Satanists hide behind their First Amendment rights and use every law that allows them to offer animals in their black masses. One Satanist told me that he raised animals for his sacrificial rituals; he is protected by the same law that allows Jews to raise animals for use in koshering meat.

In her book, Escape from Witchcraft, Roberta Blankenship writes about two girls, both Satanists, who in order to join a coven, had to renounce any belief in Christ, and had to, in a ritual, drink the blood of animals that had been skinned alive. One girl became a child of Satan in a vile blood sacrifice ceremony. She has helped defile churches and dig up bodies from fresh graves at night and sacrifice the bodies to Satan. The author goes on to say that the girls would smear blood on gravestones, smash crosses, and put flowers upside down in vases. They broke into churches, dabbed blood on the altar cloth, and burned Bibles. If anyone stumbled across them in their work, "they were in mortal danger."

Blood pacts are very common among Satanists. For example, here is one as written in the person's own blood: "My lord and master, I own you for my god. I promise to serve you while I live. From this hour I renounce all other gods and Jesus Christ and Mary and all the saints of heaven, the Catholic apostles and the Roman church and all the good will there: In any prayers which might be made by me, I promise to adore you and do you homage at least three times a day and to do the best evil I can. And to lead into evil as many persons as should be possible to me. And hatredly I renounce the Christ baptism and all the merits of Jesus Christ. And in case I should desire to change, I give you my body and soul. My life is wholly from you, having dedicated it forever, without any will to repent."

There is a prayer which reads, "Trample on crucifix, I deny the creator on heaven and earth. I deny my baptism. I deny the worship I formerly paid to God. I cleave to thee, Satan, and in thee I believe."

Many blood pacts are written in the Enochian language or in the Witch's Alphabet, or Satanic alphabet. Some are written in the Runes language, and some are composed in Latin. One particular blood pact that I was asked to decipher reads: "I am a son of Satan. Satan is forever my lord."

Another pact: "Your life is no longer in your hands. Your soul is mine." This one was done in the Satanic alphabet.

Another: "I renounce God. I renounce Christ. I will serve only Satan. To my enemies, death. To my friends, love. Hail, Satan."

One cannot become a Satanist without renouncing belief in Jesus Christ. A Satanist still can believe in God, but must deny Jesus Christ. Satan knows that the only way to the Father is through His Son, Jesus Christ.

You must note the difference in the blood mentioned in Satanists' blood pacts and the blood of Jesus that He shed on the cross. Jesus' blood was redemptive, a blood that sets one free. The blood shed in Satanic rituals represents a bondage, that binds one to Satan.

One young man told me that he drew a pentagram on his chest in his own blood whenever he worshipped Satan, the idea being that he would be able to protect himself from the demonic forces that he summoned through his worship.

The persons sent by Charles Manson to murder Sharon Tate and her friends in 1969 wrote on the walls in blood, a different use of the blood ritual. Details of their actions are given in the book, *"Helter Skelter."*

Newspaper reports on the Night Stalker killings in California show that he also wrote messages using his victims' blood. Such actions are very common in instances of sadistic ritual murders.

Satanists believe there is great power in blood, the ultimate power coming from the blood acquired in a human sacrifice. To take this a step further, the purest blood comes from the sacrifice of a child. Satanists have been known to covet blood from a newborn infant, and, as mentioned before, to use melted baby fat in making candles, which play an important role in various Satanic rituals.

Satanists are convinced that there is terrific power in blood and that by drinking blood they will be able to achieve power magnified several times.

6

Punk and Heavy Metal

Many of those who are involved in the production and distribution of punk and heavy metal music deny that the lyrics are meaningful. But that's not surprising. Would you expect the purveyors of this style of "entertainment" to confess that its intent was to lead youths into the snare of Satan? Of course not.

For instance, Brian Slagel of the independent record company Metal Blade, says he isn't bothered by the sadomasochistic, devil-worship and violent images projected by some of the bands he records and promotes. "It's all in fun," he tells those who complain about the images and lyrics his groups profess. "Condemning a band for being Satanistic is like saying Vincent Price is a Satanist because he was in those movies. It's all an act, really — they're playing out fantasies."

One of Slagel's groups is Slayer. A publicity shot for that band shows members leaning over the "bloody" body of a woman, gore oozing from the musicians' mouths. Slayer's fast and furious music is full of horrific and Satanic references.

Slagel sees the reason for heavy metal's popularity lying in its special escapist value, "There are so many problems and turmoil all over the place, and a lot of the youths are looking to get away from the daily realities. There's a lot of pent-up anger and aggression. Instead of going out and being in a gang and vandalizing places, you can go in and listen to a heavy metal band and get out all your aggressions."

But for many teenagers, it doesn't work out that way.

An example is a report from a newspaper, The (Portland) Oregonian, about 100 teenaged fans who turned out at a record store in Beaverton, Ore., to meet members of the Satanist rock band Mercyful Fate, a group from Denmark making its first tour of the United States."

Writer Dave Hogan noted, "The crowd remained quiet for three hours as the young musicians (all in their 20s) autographed records, posters and clothing.

Lead singer King Diamond has a reputation for wild antics, according to this article. "Diamond's show includes a gruesome painted face, a microphone stand constructed of human leg bones, and a large crucifix that he ignites." The Danish band has attracted attention because of Diamond's Satanist lyrics, which he says reflect his philosophy of life.

"You should act the way you feel, that's the main thing," he told the reporter.

Claiming not to be "putting down" Christianity and the Bible, Diamond said "people are not born to follow things written in books 2,000 years ago.

"Satan, to me, is not a guy with horns and a tail. To me, Satan stands for the power in the universe that keeps things in balance between good and bad," he told the newspaper.

"The underlying message is: Do what you want to do; don't just stand around," an 18-year-old fan was quoted. "Don't let the church or anyone influence you too much — make up your own mind."

One fan shouted "I love Satan" at the band. The group's drummer claimed this fan misunderstood what the band was trying to say.

"My personal philosophy is that nobody is better than you and nobody is better than anyone else," the drummer said. "Don't try to be somebody else's God."

At this point, it might be good to list some of the hundreds of heavy metal bands who have been accused of dealing in messages of Satanism, witchcraft and other deviant forms of activity.

A brief listing of such groups includes: The Apostles, Agnostic Front, Articles of Faith, Alien Sex Fiend, Bad Religion, Battalion of Saints, Corpse Grinders, Criminal Youth, Christian Death, Castration Squad (the band consists of five females), Crucifix, Condemned to Death, Catholic Discipline, Child Molesters, Church Police, Crown of Thorns, Dead Kennedys, The Damned, D.O.A., Dayglow Abortions, Flesheaters, Fall of Christianity, Graven Image, God, Icons of Filth, Leather Nun, Legal Weapon, Millions of Dead Cops, Mob Vengeance, Mission for Christ, Manson Youth, New Christ, Neon Christ, The Nuns, Rosemary's Babys, Suicidal Tendencies, Shattered Faith, Septic Death, Stillborn Christians, Sacred Order, Satan's Cheerleaders, Some Weird Sin, Sex Gang Children, Sick Pleasure, Sex Sick, Scarlet Harlot, Salvation Army, Skulls, Ultra Violence, Undead, Vice Squad, Violent Children, Voodoo Church and Wargasm.

One of the newest cult groups is Thee Temple Ov Psychick Youth (cq). To be a member, they must constantly ask the question, "Why?" to EVERYTHING.

They are told they are fighting a sexual repression war. They are told they are controlled through guilt and through politics. Leaders claim that this control is used to encourage weakness, fear and guilt.

"To be a Psychick Youth, your first requirement is your attitude. It must start here. . . Also remember you are fighting a war — a sexual repression war. Know that you and your choices are controlled through guilt. Know the youth are used and controlled through politics. Also know that this control is used in the encouragement of weakness, fear and guilt.

"Never take the easier, more popular way of action. Discipline is the key to a more positive individual. Know your motives, intentions and goals. One must recognize oneself, know your character and the might of your own strength."

This information comes from one of their publications. Such material says that a Psychick Youth is "a lone wolf. His dress and attitude is always different from the masses. The style of dress usually consists of black boots, gray or dark green combat trousers and shirt, black or gray jackets affixed with Psychick Cross patches. There also are Psychick Cross earrings and tattoos on the upper right arm, containing individual touches.

The haircut is a shaven head with a monk-like tail of long hair on the back of the skull, symbolizing discipline and sensuality. It is not uncommon to find members of the Psychick Youth wearing a steel ring that pierces the penis or labia.

Steel rings or pins are sometimes worn through a member's nipples.

Members of the musical group Psychic TV have all of the above. They also engage in rituals. The group has played in the United States three times. Their show in Boston in 1984 began at 11 p.m., the 23rd hour of the day, and ran into the following morning, which was Easter. The band set up three screens, one showing Charles Manson and Jim Jones. Another depicted sex rituals, penis piercing and religious ikons. The center screen, which was larger than the two flanking it, showed scenes of self-mutilation and of a person being castrated.

The Boston Globe's story about the concert said the band was led by Genesis P-Orridge and John Gosling, two Britishers who also are active in leadership of Thee Temple Ov Psychick

Youth. Wrote critic Jim Sullivan: "You know you're in for a rough evening when the cacophony that begins the performance forces you to thrust your forefingers into your ears. When the video presentation begins 15 minutes later, there's no doubt. The first film depicts a castration." Sullivan adds this comment: "It was two hours in a torture chamber."

The Globe story continued, "Dark and doomy expressionism is one thing. An obsessive, brutal, repulsive assault of sado-masochism is another. Sunday's multiscreen display of horrific sex and violence made the gorge rise, driving numerous persons from the theater into the lobby. The video grotesquerie ranged from images of Charles Manson and Jim Jones to scenes of self-mutilation and self-immolation . . . It was no fun and it was no joke. If hell has an audio-video department, Psychic TV are its programmers.

"The Temple's stated goal is to 'mimic normal media, writing, art, sound, TV' and mutilate it. They strive to 'create a modern occult philosophy of life.' Their art, P-Orridge explained after the show, is 'a modern primitivism,' dealing with 'perversion, sexuality, conditioning and control.' "

Sullivan's article concludes, "Psychic TV's aim is shock treatment. They push tolerance over the edge, wallowing in aural abrasion and video horror. The effect is numbing and defeating, sad and sacrilegious. . ."

At the Boston concert, many of the heavy metal fans attending fled the concert hall and ran into the lobby in horror at the sights they witnessed on the screens.

Basically, Temple of the Psychick Youth indulges in sex magic, another form of cult practice.

This group is just one form of cults involved in heavy metal music. Heavy metal has become a major concern for law enforcement agencies across the United States. Devotees of heavy metal music have been reported to have been involved in grave robbing, all types of perverted sex, animal sacrifices and, in some cases, gruesome violence is the goal. As you can see from the example of the Psychick Youth, gruesome violence such as penis piercing and castration are practiced.

One former Satanist told me that he had broken every one of the Ten Commandments except the one that forbids murder. He told me that he worshipped Satan and had asked for the power to commit murder. This young man received the force he sought, as he later murdered the person he had intended to kill. It is my belief that young people become involved in heavy metal violence because it teaches them to be anti-social. As we can see from the Psychick Youth cult, it teaches them to become violent. It tells them to commit murder, to offer sacrifices.

Another notorious musician, Ozzy Osbourne, has a song called "War Pigs." The title of the song indicates that Osbourne himself is anti-social. In the song, Osbourne makes the statement in his lyrics, "Just like witches at black masses." The average person would not understand what this message conveyed, but one involved in Satanism would.

This is what Ozzy Osbourne is singing about in "War Pigs." "Just like witches at black masses" is a training tool for young heavy metal fans that choose the left-hand path of Satanism.

Another heavy metal musician totally fascinated with the image of death is Alice Cooper. In his song, "Cold Ethel," he sings about having sex with a corpse. Part of the lyric says, "No lie, Ethel's as frigid as an Eskimo Pie. She's cool in bed and she oughta be, 'cause Ethel's dead." Basically, the song seems to advocate necrophilia, having sex with a corpse. Such an act is not uncommon among non-traditional Satanists. Many of the cults ARE having sex with the dead. As one case described it, a man had sex with a girl's corpse on several occasions, until the body was discovered by authorities.

Heavy metal groups are involved in sex magic, which involves all different types of perverted sex.

It is important that parents as well as law enforcement agents understand that heavy metalists are a very dangerous breed.

The National Coalition on TV Violence issued a report that rock music TV videos not only illustrate violent song lyrics but also injected additional violence, much of it sexual in nature. This watchdog group reported that in 1983 song lyrics mentioned violence an average of 8.5 times per hour.

One rock video show carried by the MTV network, however, averaged 18 instances of violence per hour. One news article reads: "Police blame cult murder on rock videos," In part, the story said a 17-year-old was tortured and murdered by a teen-aged cult of Satan worshippers involved in rock videos that glorified Satanic rituals, the very factor in the youth's death.

Another report says, "Rock music inspires suicide." A Texas coach found a sophomore boy hanging by a rope attached to a football stadium stand. Nearby, the coach discovered a cassette tape player. The player contained a tape of AC-DC's recording, "Highway to Hell." The victim had told a friend the night before that he was "going to be with Satan."

The AC-DC musician who wrote the lyrics for "Highway to Hell," Bon Scott, is pictured on the cover of that particular album wearing a pentagram around his neck. He is laughing.

He sings the song: "Hey, Satan, paid my dues playing in a rocking band. Hey, mama, look at me, I'm on my way to the promised land, on that highway to Hell."

Bon Scott died in the back seat of an auto. He choked to death on his own vomit.

The term AC-DC has several meanings, of course. Probably the most recognizable is the lightning bolt that separates the AC from the DC. It is symbolic of Satan. It is also the same lightning bolt that used as an insignia on the collars of members of Hitler's storm troops.

United Press International, on Jan. 14, 1986, reported that "Ozzy Osbourne's lyrics were cited as the cause of a suicide." That was what the headlines read. Osbourne's song, "Suicide Solution," was allegedly the reason for the young man's death.

The story goes on to point out that a 19-year-old shot himself to death with his father's gun after listening to Osbourne's albums for several hours. The article says the suicide victim was still wearing stereo headphones when his body was found.

Part of the song "Suicide Solution" says, "Breaking laws, knocking doors, but there's no one at home. Made your bed, rest your head, but you lie there and moan. Where to hide, suicide is the only way out."

Battle Cry Publications of Chino, Calif., in June 1984 reported, "Satan worship rituals on the increase." The article continued that "animal mutilations and grave robbing are increasingly common as rock music groups such as Judas Priest and Motley Crue scream instructions for Satanic rituals.

"A Hollywood High School student wearing metal-studded leather brace bands and a Judas Priest cap told a local newspaper, 'I often think of Satan as a cool dude, since he controls one part of the supernatural. He tends to let you be on your own, to do what you want. God has His own rules on how you're supposed to live. They're kind of binding. He wants to put you into a jail cell to control you.'

"This young man has admitted that he has drawn a pentagram with dead animals' blood. It's supposed to give Satan his praise. You burn them or dismember them (the animals) inside this pentagram.

"Detectives believe that the biggest promoter of Satanism today is heavy metal music. The kids are getting all kinds of messages in the music."

Variety, the respected entertainment trade weekly publication, reported on Dec, 31, 1986, that the British heavy metal group Judas Priest, "accused of selling records that allegedly led two Sparks, Nevada youths to shoot themselves, will face a trial. Washoe District Judge Jerry Whitehead has ordered attorneys to set a trial date after denying a defense motion to dismiss the suit against the group." The case was expected to be tried in the fall of 1987.

Variety continued, "A lawsuit was filed by victim James M. Vance and the mother of Raymond Eugene Belknap, 18, who died in the Dec. 23, 1985, shotgun blast; Vance was left severely disfigured.

"The suit claims that Judas Priest and CBS Records are responsible for the two youths shooting themselves in the head in a church parking lot after spending six hours listening to an album by the band. They claim the music intentionally had a hypnotic effect on its listeners and the lyrics could lead young people with emotional problems to reject society and commit suicide.

" 'The suggestive lyrics combined with the continuous beat and rhythmic non-changing intonation of the music combined to induce, encourage, aid, abet and otherwise mesmerize the plaintiff into believing the answer to life was death,' attorney Kenneth McKenna wrote in the lawsuit.

"Lawyers for the band argued in the motion that they were protected from a lawsuit by their Constitutional rights to freedom of expression. They also claimed there was no basis in the suit for which the band could be held liable for damages.

" 'What this means is we're going to trial and will surely get a decision on this important Constitutional issue in Reno prior to anywhere else,' says McKenna.

"A similar California suit against hard rocker Ozzy Osbourne and CBS Records recently was dismissed by a judge. Consequently, the Reno case might be the first to go to trial.

"In his ruling, Whitehead did not address the freedom of speech issue or merits of the case. He said under Nevada law a lawsuit could not be dismissed unless every factual claim made by the plaintiff could be considered true and there could still be no basis for damages.

"McKenna said Belknap and Vance had been listening to the album 'Stained Glass' in Belknap's bedroom. He said they had been drinking 'some' and smoking marijuana."

The group Venom, on their album cover, makes it quite clear whom they serve. They say, "The death of you God we demand. And we spit on the virgin you worship and sit at Lord Satan's left hand." Is it any wonder that many of our young people are involved in sadistic murders, diabolic acts, mutilations, killing of parents, brothers and sisters and necrophilia? The only thing that heavy metal does is oppose authority and encourage those who follow it to rebel against parents, against police, against all types of religious leaders and school personnel. Heavy metal groups teach those who follow them to "do their own thing." Basically, their message is pure humanism. If it feels good, do it. There are no absolutes at all.

There is a song entitled "Possessed," which says, "Look at me, Satan's child. Born of evil, thus defiled. Brought to life through Satanic birth. Come look at me and I'll show you things that will open your eyes. Listen to me and I'll tell you things that will sicken your mind. I drink the vomit of the priest, make love with the dying whore. Satan is my master incarnate. Hail, praise to my unholy host."

You be the judge. Are such groups ambassadors for Satan?

One group that has been actively fighting heavy metal and punk music is the Back in Control Training Center in Fullerton, Calif. For the past dozen years, this center has offered a system of parenting designed to help parents assert their rights to set and enforce rules of behavior for their children.

The *Los Angeles Times* reported that organizers of the center believe music is an important factor in the corruption of today's youth.

"To a lot of people, punk and heavy metal is a fad, here today and gone tomorrow," said Darlyne Pettincchio, associate director of the center. She told the newspaper, "For some kids that's true. For other kids, it becomes a way of life that changes their value systems and beliefs."

The center's director, Greg Bodenhamer, is a former deputy

probation officer in Orange County, Calif. He is the author of a book, Back in Control: How to Get Your Children to Behave. (Prentice-Hall, 1983).

Bodenhamer told a conference of parents, teachers, counselors, probation officers and police officers in Anaheim, Calif, recently that "one of the worst problems we work with on a continuing basis is kids in punk or heavy metal music.

"It's rare that a week passes that we don't have one or two metalers come in to the center; we see fewer punkers, four or five a month. Over the course of a year, you're looking at dozens and dozens of kids," he told a reporter for the *Times*.

"It's when they start to dress it and act it that it becomes a problem," he said. "When the parents reach us, more often than not, their kids have developed serious problems at school. Their grades have dropped; there is chronic tardiness and truancy; they have a real disinterest in school.

"There's also a very quick drawing away from the family. Once kids become part of the heavy metal or punk culture, there is an attitude they frequently pass on to the parents: 'I'm going to do what I want; the hell with you, leave me alone,' and with the metalers, in particular, better than 90 percent are involved with drugs."

Pettinicchio, in addition to her work with the Back in Control Training Center, has been a deputy probation officer for more than a decade and serves as a punk and heavy metal consultant to the California Youth Authority, as well as police and probation departments throughout California. She says that in her experience, the kids involved in heavy metal and punk music "usually are of average intelligence and are very capable of doing what they want in whatever they choose to do in life—if they were motivated in that direction." She says she finds that most of them have poor self-images. Sometimes, they're outcasts, people who aren't in step with their peers.

"All the kids we've dealt with are seeking a place to belong," she says. "The other thing is they're bored and seeking excitement. Heavy metal or punk is exciting. You never know what's going to happen.

"The other thing we've found is there is very little parental control. A lot of times their parents really don't know what their kids are involved in. They don't know who they're associating with, and they don't know what they're doing."

She told the Los Angeles paper, "They are angry kids and punk and heavy metal becomes an acceptable release for their anger."

Heavy metal music evolved from the late '60s and early '70s hard rock bands such as Led Zeppelin, The Doors, Cream and Jimi Hendrix. Pettinicchio says the music, which often contains Satanic messages, is exremely important to a heavy metaler. "They refer to the band members as their saints and sometimes their gods. They look up to them, they idolize them."

Officer Paul Henisey of the Newport Beach, Calif., Police Department's juvenile section says Newport police have arrested punkers for crimes ranging from disturbances and vandalism to assault and battery and attempted murder. In 1984, they arrested four teenagers for the vandalism and theft of an urn from a cemetery. The youths, he says, had been holding black masses and making pretend sacrifices on a sand pit in upper Newport bay, which they had labeled "Devil's Island."

"For a lot of kids, punk or heavy metal is teenage rebellion," Henisey told a conference in Anaheim. "For others, it's not. The problem is where do you draw the line? Where does the harmless aspect of it end and the harmful aspect of it begin? That's the difficult part."

Bodenhamer says that "No kid who is into punk or heavy metal will admit he or she has a problem. They will tell you that you don't understand, that you're making a big deal out of nothing. For some kids that's true, but there is no way to tell which kids will breach the barrier from it being a game to the point where it becomes serious. And our

98

recommendation is don't let kids be into punk; don't let them be into heavy metal."

The Back In Control program, Bodenhamer says, calls upon Parents to establish what he calls the "mandatory rule"—a rule the child has literally no choice but to obey.

Bodenhamer says most adults agree on many of the mandatory rules for children. "Should children be given a choice as to whether they use illegal drugs or not, or should we decide for them that they're not going to? Should kids be able to hit mom or dad, or should we decide for them they're not going to?

Bodenhamer explains that a mandatory rule has three parts to it. He says the rule must be clearly stated, with parents telling the child what to do, when to do it and how often or how long to do it. Next, there should be an effective follow-through to ensure that the rule is obeyed. "Supervision is an absolute necessity in keeping kids out of punk and heavy metal and keeping them away from drugs and alcohol and making sure they're going to school every day and that they're coming home on time."

Third, he says, there must be consistency. When the parents consistently follow through, the child begins to internalize the rule, Bodenhamer tells parents that they make a mistake when they get angry about their childrens' behavior.

"When we focus on each other, we lose control of the rule. Does a 15-year-old punker care that you resent something? Kids into punk and heavy metal, especially, and almost always kids into drugs, are hooked into this power struggle."

Bodenhamer says the Back To Control Center urges "argument deflection." Use the words "regardless" or "nevertheless" when, for example, a child says, "If you didn't hate me, you'd let me go to the concert." The parent should answer, "Regardless of whether I hate you or not, you're not going to the concert."

Getting a child out of the heavy metal culture requires taking specific steps such as eliminating all the records, clothing and friends associated with the lifestyle.

"If you don't totally de-punk or de-metal a kid, if they're already into it, they will hold onto that little bit they have left just as tenaciously as if you let them hold onto everything; and they will still see it as a part of their being. The whole thing has to go."

The most alarming thing about teenagers' devotion to punk and heavy metal music, according to Pettinicchio, is their fascination with Satan.

"Not all automatically buy into this system," she told the Santa Barbara, Calif., *News-Press*, "but we're finding an increasing number involved in devil worship, priding themselves on communicating through occult symbols that most of us wouldn't even notice.

"They greet each other with the sign of Satan, a hand sign made by closing the fist and extending the index and little fingers. The fingers that are up represent the devil's horns and the three fingers down represent a denial of the Trinity (Father, Son and Holy Spirit)."

She says she attended a concert where the entire audience, encouraged by the rock group, waved their hands in this position.

7

Dungeons and Dragons

In October of 1986, Patricia Pulling of Richmond, Va., issued an 8 x 10 booklet of more than 80 pages. Its title was a simple one: "Articles Relating to Dungeons and Dragons." Inside its pages are reproductions of newspaper and magazine clippings from across the country, the overwhelming majority of which condemn this fantasy role-playing game. In my own investigations of the occult over the past dozen years, I have heard time and again of youngsters who have let their imaginations get away from them, possibly because of the influence of this game. Patricia Pulling founded the group called B.A.D.D. (Bothered About D. & D.) in 1983, after the death of her 16-year-old son. She says that his suicide was "directly related" to the game of Dungeons & Dragons, a registered trademark for the fantasy game marketed by TSR, Inc. of Lake Geneva, Wis.

Mrs. Pulling says that B.A.D.D. is "an organization dedicated to educating the public on the harmful effects of entertainment violence which is occurring and growing in our society. We are concerned with violent forms of entertainment such as: violent-occult related rock music; role-playing games that utilize occult mythology and the worship of occult gods in role playing situations like Dungeons & Dragons; teen Satanism involving murder and suicide, and pornography as it is affecting adolescent behavior and reshaping attitudes and values in a negative manner."

She continues, "Our hopes are to be influential in the restoration of respect for human life."

B.A.D.D. serves as an informational outlet for law enforcement agencies, schools, churches, doctors, lawyers, psychiatrists, social workers and others. The group has had presentations on "60 Minutes" and "The 700 Club." Activities of the group have been written about in the *Chicago Tribune, USA Today* and *Newsweek.*

"B.A.D.D. also acts as a referral system for people who need help regarding entertainment violence issues," Mrs. Pulling says. "We believe that the problem is not only a lack of information but many times misinformation. We feel that if we all work together we can improve our society for our children."

Those who may be interested in the group, which is a nonprofit, voluntary organization enjoying tax-exempt status, may contact it at this address: B.A.D.D. Inc. , P.O. Box 5513, Richmond, Va, 23220. The phone number is 1-804-264-0403.

In 1985 the National Coalition on Television Violence (NCTV), which is headquartered in Washington, D.C., issued a press release that charged that at least nine suicides and murders had occurred in which Dungeons & Dragons "has been a major factor in causing." (More recent figures from NCTV place the number of deaths at 70-plus.)

The group NCTV called for "required warnings on all D&D game books and for counter advertising to inform the public about the deadly effects."

Evidence presented was based on police and newspaper reports as well as interviews with family members. "These document a pattern of youths becoming deeply involved in D&D, a fantasy role-playing game that involves constant attack and counter-attack. Suicide notes and numerous details connecting the deaths with the game have been found with the bodies," the press release recounted.

The release listed the names of eight of the victims (the other being withheld at the request of the family). One of the victims was Mrs. Pulling's son, Irving Lee, who died on June 9, 1982 after shooting himself through the heart. The suicide occurred just hours after a D&D curse was placed on him during a game conducted at his local high school.

Mrs. Pulling said, "The large majority of the information in D&D manuals is violence-oriented. It consists of detailed descriptions of killings, including human sacrifice, assassination, sadism, premeditated murder, and curse of insanity. Much of the material comes from demonology including witchcraft, the occult, and evil monsters. The game details multiple curses of insanity including suicidal and homicidal mania."

Mrs. Pulling quoted from the "Dungeon Master's Guide," stating that the game "details sado-masochism, homicidal mania, and delusional insanity in similar ways. It encourages players to put themselves in the roles of their characters." She said the instruction book calls on Dungeon Masters to take on the role of an insane character when madness occurs, since most players would not be willing to go that far.

D&D is played in groups under the direction of a dungeon master who has designed the dungeons and the hostile forces that will be encountered. It is primarily played by males, ages 12 to 20, and is one of many similar war and mystical fantasy games available.

NCTV estimates that there are from three to four million players in the U.S. The game can last for months and even years, with the goal being not to get killed and to accumulate as much power as possible. Power is earned, the NCTV says, by the murder of enemies and monsters, etc. The players grow in power until they can achieve even demi-god status. Players can be "good" or "evil" and develop in each game as it progresses. Players are encouraged to identify with their own character in the game. It is common in schools that some players prefer to be called by their D&D names. The game entails various attacks, assassinations, spying, theft, and poisonings. An extreme number of monsters from horror and demonology are involved including 22 types of Satanic demons and devils. Combat armor, medieval weaponry, spells and curses, and many forms of mental attack are involved. Holy/unholy water, magic of all types, flying carpets and brooms, charms, ESP, mental telepathy and wizards fill the game. Players can be cursed with 20 different types of insanity.

Dr. Thomas Radecki, a psychiatrist at the University of Illinois School of Medicine and chairman of NCTV, said, "The evidence in these cases is really quite impressive. There is no doubt in my mind that the game Dungeons & Dragons is causing young men to kill themselves and others. This game is one of non-stop combat and violence. Although I am sure that the people at TSR mean no harm, that is exactly what their games are causing. Based on player interviews and game materials, it is clear to me that this game is desensitizing players to violence, and, also, causing an increased tendency to violent behavior.

"While TSR, with its millions of dollars in profits, can find some psychologists and psychiatrists to applaud its violence, nine out of ten expert aggression researchers with whom I have spoken about this game, expressed concern. All ten stated that, in their opinions, based on entertainment violence research, the playing of violent games does cause an increased tendency toward violent behavior in many participants."

Dr. Radecki has criticized psychologist Dr. Joyce Brothers

for becoming a paid spokesperson for Dungeons & Dragons. Dr. Brothers has been quoted, "I reflect for the company what's going on in people's lives. The game is very interesting to me because it is a cooperative game." Dr. Radecki responds to this statement: "While Dungeons & Dragons is a game of cooperation and working together, that cooperation involves cooperating in violence, premeditated murder, and war. While it does stimulate creative fantasies, these fantasies are of killing and horror. There is a need to get the honest information out to the American people. The research is overwhelming that violent entertainment is having a harmful effect on its participants. The changes are most often gradual and subtle. Few become murderers, but many become more aggressive. When a children's game is documented to cause many deaths, it should not be promoted through advertising and cartoon programming. (The CBS television network broadcast a cartoon version of "Dungeons & Dragons") The cartoon, although it contains some prosocial behavior and is, often, not as intense as the game, still averages over 50 acts of violence per hour. It promotes fantasies of violence and teaches the use of violence as normal problem-solving behavior. D&D teaches the player to see the enemy as hideously evil and with whom violence is usually the only effective way of relating."

Mrs. Pulling and NCTV asked the Federal Trade Commission to require warnings on the covers of all Dungeons & Dragons books to warn that it has caused a number of suicides and murders. They also sought required counter advertising whenever D&D is being promoted to warn viewers and asked immediate research funding by Congress into the impact of other violent games on players, to help resolve any doubts and to guide public action.

Ron Slaby, a psychologist at Harvard University and national expert on the causes of violence in children, has said, "The research evidence we do have points in the opposite direction of the statements of certain psychologists and psychiatrists who see D&D as harmless or even good. The popularity of violent toys and games in our society may be a sign of our own desensitization to aggression and its effects. I am amazed at how involved in violence young people are these days. The large majority of parents are not careful to keep these models of violence from coming into our homes."

And here's a statement from Dr. Arnold Goldstein, director of the Center for Research on Aggression at the University of Syracuse: "Like many other psychologists, I feel quite negatively about violent toys and violent play. With desensitization effects that start with childhood games, we help make violence a part of the American lifestyle, I think it's a bad idea to play a violent role-playing game, such as Dungeons & Dragons. For many, such play causes subtle changes, which increase both a desensitization toward violence and a tendency to commit aggressive behavior. We, psychologists, use role-playing in therapy, as I've been researching for 15 years, to bring about good effects. I must assume that the same teaching of destructive behavior will have harmful effects. There are over 150 studies on the effects of role-playing on attitudes and behavior changes in teaching positive behavior. There is every reason to suspect that the role-playing of anti-social behavior will increase its probability of occurrence, especially when the behavior is practiced and rewarded as in a game-playing situation."

This comes from Dr. John P. Murray, a psychologist at Boys Town in Nebraska and an editor of the original Surgeon General's study of the effects of TV violence: "The effect of being involved with aggressive symbols is an increased tendency to anger and violence in real life. A violent role-playing game would reinforce aggressive behavior. We routinely discourage violent games and violent play. I encourage parents not to buy violent toys or games for their children since these increase violent fantasies and the tendencies toward violence."

Here is a portion of a letter written by Pat Dempsey of Lutz, Fla. His son, Michael, committed suicide in the spring of 1981, after becoming deeply involved in Dungeons & Dragons.

"Mike had no mental problems prior to playing the game," Dempsey wrote. "A junior and senior high student introduced him to the game. They were playing the game during school and after. His whole life began to revolve around a game I knew little about.

"He asked me to make real medieval weapons. I refused. Unknown to me he had made his own which could inflict injury. His demeanor started to change in a very subtle manner. When he was asked to do chores around the house, he would walk by me as if he was in another world.

"After his death I found out from his fellow D&D players that they were into astro-projection as outlined in the D&D book. They were into casting spells. Fantasy in his mind turned into reality. He began to cast spells at home directed toward his mother. He was using sulfur and garlic to conjure up demons (outlined in the D&D book) in his room. His interest in home activities ceased. He unemotionally told his mother one day he no longer loved her. We were taken aback — shocked. He spent about 95 percent of his time in his room working on D&D and very little time was spent on school work. He was obtaining the power that the game promises and it became foremost in his life.

". . . He become another person, his voice changed to a deep gutteral sound. His face became somewhat twisted and his eyes were glazed as he screamed at me that he was going to finish his D&D program. In the next second, his voice was normal and very quietly he told me that he had to work on his D&D program to get a good grade. I didn't know the boy sitting next to me. There is no doubt in my mind that he came under the influence of demonic forces. He killed himself directly after this conversation. We did not realize at the time that by becoming involved in D&D it could lead to a sudden depression and to death. . ."

The files of B.A.D.D. are filled with information about the deaths of young people who were involved with Dungeons & Dragons. In Arlington, Texas, James A. Stalley, a 17-year-old senior at Arlington High School, pulled a .410 gauge sawed-off shotgun from a briefcase and shot himself in the temple, in full view of his drama class. *United Press International* reported in January 1985, that Stalley was described as an intellectual who enjoyed the game Dungeons & Dragons.

In Oakland, Calif., the *Associated Press* reported another case in January 1985, when a 15-year-old boy shot his 14-year-old brother while playing D&D. Police said the two were "playing a game that deals heavily with fantasy death and used a gun as a kind of prop. The younger boy, Juan Decarlos Kimbrough, had assumed the role of 'dungeon master.' He died. A police lieutenant said, "I'm told that to die in combat while playing the game is nothing because there are spells which can be cast to bring you back . . . Unfortunately, that's not the way it works in real life."

In February 1985, Jeffrey Jacklovich of Topeka, Kansas killed himself with a revolver. He was 14. He left a note that said, "I want to go to the world of elves and fantasy and leave the world of conflict."

Two young brothers, Daniel and Steven Erwin, died in November 1984 in an apparent death pact. The youths, 16 and 12, lived in Lafayette, Colo. Police said the younger boy killed his brother and then took his own life with a .22 caliber pistol. Authorities said they believed the death pact was a part of the game of D&D. A detective's report read, "No doubt, D&D cost them their lives."

Three youngsters in Ragland, Ala. were arrested in 1985 and charged in the murder of a female convenience store clerk. Two of the youths were 17 at the time, the third only 14. The link among the three, police told the *Associated Press*, was

Dungeons & Dragons. One of the trio was urged by friends to burn the game after an evangelist told them the devil inspired the violent, imaginary plots involving medieval monsters. The youth called his friends "religious fanatics" and declared himself to be an atheist.

Two Chicago area teenagers were found murdered in a Colorado mountain wilderness in mid-1985. Police said that books from a fantasy game called Villains & Vigilantes were found at the site where the bodies of a 15-year-old girl and 16-year-old boy were discovered. The couple had run away from their Illinois home a week earlier, after telling friends they planned to marry.

The principal suspect in their deaths, a 15-year-old friend who had run away with them, was described by police as an avid player of Dungeons & Dragons since the sixth grade.

Danny Remeta claimed an eight-state crime spree he went on in 1985 was inspired by D&D. Remeta was apprehended in Kansas after a three-week reign of terror. Remeta and a partner, William Dunn, were charged with murder after two men were abducted from a grain elevator in Kansas and killed execution-style. In an interview with reporters from the *Detroit News* and the *Detroit Free Press*, Remeta said the killings were inspired by Dungeons & Dragons.

"Have you ever heard of Dungeons & Dragons?" he asked reporters. "That had a lot to do with it. . . It's not just a board game. It's a lot deeper than a board game. I've got five friends that are locked up for the same thing (murder) right now (because of the game)," he told them.

One of the friends Remeta named was James Gainforth, convicted in the death of a gas station clerk in Traverse City, Mich.

The *News* said that Remeta provided the paper with a handwritten note that read, in part:

"I now hear the hiss of my dragon's rage,
For he, too, is locked into a cage.

He'll patiently wait for another to rise like me.
He'll be fed and again shall rise ever so free,
The game another shall carry on, for we can't all fall.
My treasure is becoming part of the dragon forever.
Many shall die who strive to find our hidden treasure,
But someone shall play our game for all do seek a treasure."

In Fremont, Calif., a 14-year-old girl was found murdered alongside a road, her head wrapped in two green garbage bags. Two days before her death, she wrote a class essay entitled, "Dungeons & Dragons," in which she wrote, "I like playing Dungeons & Dragons while I'm stoned, because it's such a head trip. When I am high and playing . . . I can really get into the game. I can almost see the Orcas coming after me and a spell being cast on me. It's so realistic, I begin to feel like a medieval warrior in a cold damp dungeon fighting for power, gold and glory. I might get a little carried away at times, but I finally come back to earth."

According to B.A.D.D., the girl's killer still runs loose with no clues other than that she was the victim of a ritualistic murder.

In Trenton, N.J., a mother has waged a years-long fight to find out what happened to her 13-year-old son, who inhaled lethal chloroform and died in March of 1983. Winifred Phillips believes that Dungeons & Dragons may have played a role in the death of her son Michael. The youngster was a dungeon master and played the game twice daily with some of his classmates at the prestigious American Boychoir School. His mother said he played during an afternoon rest period and prior to going to bed. Authorities said young Phillips died during an afternoon rest period. Police tried to determine if the boy's death was accidental or intentional. The boy's mother said she did not believe that it was accidental, nor did she think it was a suicide.

In Watertown, N.Y., police reported that a 15-year-old boy was "researching" Dungeons & Dragons when he pointed a shotgun at the head of his ll-year-old friend. The gun fired and the younger child died. A police captain said that the boy "was doing research regarding the game, in his own mind, at the time of the crime." The policeman said the boy was an "enthusiast" of the game. An attorney hired to represent the boy said, however, that the shooting had nothing to do with the game and that it was accidental. State police said the shooting was intentional.

In Angleton, TX., a former prison psychologist was found guilty of raping a 15-year-old girl. He was sentenced to nine years in prison and the case is on appeal. Police said the man and his wife used the game Dungeons & Dragons to entice the girl into having sex.

The girl testified that she had played the game at the home of Armondo Simon, 33. She said she often took on the role of "someone who would lose their powers after doing something wrong." In the game Simon would act out the part of a character constantly interested in women, while his wife, Angela, 21, would often play the role of a lesbian, the girl told a trial jury.

Simon or his wife usually played the dungeon master, in control of the game, the girl testified. The prosecuting attorney said the Simons and the girl often played the game while drinking alcohol. The prosecutor said the intention was to strip the girl's inhibitions and encourage her to have sex with Simon.

The first time the girl had sexual intercourse with Simon was in his car while they parked along a road while returning from a Dungeons & Dragons convention in Houston, she testified.

Simon had been employed as a psychologist by the Texas Department of Corrections, counseling inmates serving sentences for sexual crimes. He was fired after being charged with rape.

The St. Petersburg (Fla.) Times in 1986 completed an

intensive investigation of the death of Louis Solomon, 15. The youth died in a police car after he held a gun to his head for three hours during a standoff with police in Pinellas Park, Fla. In his brief life, Solomon lived in five cities and attended eight schools. He often was in a juvenile delinquency program, a hospital or a mental health facility. State social workers said the youngster had an IQ of 150 and was described as a "whiz at computers." Those who knew the young man said he was confused about his religious beliefs and sometimes talked about devil worship. The youth's stepfather said that the boy's problems began when Solomon was 12 and became fascinated with Dungeons & Dragons.

Solomon's stepfather told the newspaper, "He started hanging around kids down the street who were playing Dungeons & Dragons. Immediately after that, no more school work, no more homework, misbehaving. He wouldn't listen; he wanted to play the game."

The stepfather told reporters that Solomon once tried to commit suicide when he tried to take game materials away from him.

Solomon and a friend had escaped from a juvenile detention facility. When the two were apprehended by police, an officer got out of the car; and at that point, Solomon pulled a .22 caliber revolver from his pants. He put the gun to his head, then put the barrel into his mouth. He allowed a companion to leave the car. For three hours, officers and mental health workers tried to convince him to surrender. Finally a police sergeant fired two darts from an electric stun gun. At the same time, Solomon pulled the trigger of the revolver. Death came.

An Annapolis, Md., psychologist, Diane Pizzirusso, has been reported to have serious reservations about D&D. Pizzirusso is a Christian counselor who says she offers therapy from a Christian viewpoint. She told the *Baltimore News-American* that "most of the activities focus on violence and revenge and thievery and those kinds of things. And so many kids get so wrapped up, they walk around talking about the game all the time. Their grades drop — that's all they talk about."

Pizzirusso said she had seen "actual personality changes" in children. "It's usually the sensitive kids, shy or maybe not succsssful in other areas, who attach to the game. They get off on the sense of power and control and get more vicious verbally — talking of revenge."

She told of counseling youngsters who had broken into a house, with the idea of stealing items to raise enough money to buy expensive accessories for the game.

"They described the crime as part of the game," she told the newspaper. "These were kids with absolutely sparkling records, who just said, 'Gee, we were just playing a game.' "

After the *News-American* and the *Baltimore Sun* published articles about the D&D controversy over allowing the game to be played in schools, Pat Pulling wrote a letter to the editors of the two papers.

"Many children who have played this 'game,' and have had emotional problems as a result of their involvement with this game, had never been children with any emotional problems or 'weaknesses' prior to playing this game," she wrote.

"The research that has been done by credible professionals, involved in ten years of research on the effects of media violence and violent forms of entertainment such as: violence in movies, television violence, violent videos (MTV and arcade games), and violent fantasy role playing games, supports the belief that healthy individuals exposed to violent entertainment will suffer increased aggressiveness in their behavior. The degree of aggressiveness will depend upon the individual's participation in situations of stress as well as the type of stress."

Mrs. Pulling contends that the game stresses evil over good. "The evil characters are able to achieve far more power than the good characters, with encouraging deviousness in order to achieve more wealth, power and longevity of life in each game. Many times players will kill a character or close friend's character only to avoid sharing jointly acquired treasure. This is justifiable in the name of the game. However, this is just one type of unacceptable, unhealthy behavior promoting unethical values that occur within this game."

James Bolgiano, a psychologist at Odessa High School in Texas, says that fantasy games were seen a decade ago as providing a healthy outlet for some kids as an experience in role-playing. But now, he notes, many players of the fantasy games — especially Dungeons & Dragons — are having trouble coping in the classroom and other places.

"In my opinion, it's related to the game. D&D is not like Monopoly. The game lasts for days, weeks — whatever. These characters have powers and a personality of their own, and sometimes the personality of the character becomes tangled with the actual person."

A former player, Kevin Porter, told the *Odessa American* that he agreed with Bolgiano's views. "Some players I knew believed they were wizards or assassins, and years from now, if I hear these people have mental problems, I won't be surprised."

In Birmingham, Ala., a 14-year-old boy played hooky from school and played Dungeons & Dragons in the city's sewers for four hours. He told police that he felt no fear in the pitch-black underground tunnel about the nine-foot-tall trolls and other creatures that were down there.

The boy said he was a "magic fighter user," possessing supernatural powers to protect him from "men who turn into animals." He said that "in this game you're not yourself. You become another person, with weapons and magic to use, I had dreams about it, and today the dream didn't stop when I woke up."

He said he had stopped playing the game several times over

a four-year period, but always went back because it was "so exciting." His mother said she thought the game was dangerous because her son thought of little else. She said she wanted other parents to realize how addicting the game could be.

The mother told a writer for the *Birmingham News* that she gave in to her son playing the game with friends "because he's never been a minute's trouble." When school officials called to tell her that her son wasn't in classes, she found a hand-drawn map in his bedroom.

At the bottom of the map, the youngster had written, "I have gone to the dungeon. The dungeon master will aid me, so don't worry. Find Elork and tell him to follow this map and meet me inside." He signed the note "Kelf," the name he used in the game. Elork was the name used by a friend with whom he played D&D. The map also referred to "lizard man, the moss wasteland of trolls and a hunting ground for werewolves." The youngster said he wasn't afraid to play in the sewer, but admitted that "today maybe the game went too far for me."

When parents objected to the Putnam, Conn. school board allowing D&D to be played at the school, a member of the board told the *New York Times*, "There are more important things on the agenda than Dungeons & Dragons — mathematics, reading or smoking, for example." A board member said, "My daughter played D&D since she was 26, and she is now happily married. There is no evidence that links D&D to suicide."

The controversy erupted in Putnam when a 13-year-old boy committed suicide in April, 1984. Opponents of D&D said the youth had played the game regularly at the Putnam Library.

School boards around the country have banned the game, believing that impressionable teenagers cannot handle the violent role playing and occult imagery.

In a meeting with the Putnam school board, a minister told the group, "You have authorized Russian roulette." The Rev.

Robert O. Bakke of the Faith Bible Evangelical Church said, "Over the months to come there will be many thrilling and harmless clicks of the gun as Dungeons & Dragons is held to the heads of our young people. But another deadly explosion will come."

However, the chairman of the Putnam school board said that banning the game could be construed as censorship and as violating the students' rights.

The CBS television program "60 Minutes" produced a segment about the Dungeons & Dragons controversy. The story was first broadcast in September 1985.

Mrs. Pulling, her husband and daughter Melissa were interviewed by "60 Minutes" correspondent Ed Bradley. Melissa Pulling, 12 at the time of the interview, told Bradley that her late brother "Bink" had once threatened to kill her. The threat was unknown to her parents until after the boy committed suicide in 1983. It was believed he made the threat because of his involvement with D&D.

Gary Gygax, who created the game, appeared on the show and said that there is "no evidence to show more than a coincidental" linkage between the game and any deaths. He asserted that evidence gathered by the game's opponents is "as unscientific as you can get," adding that it is "nothing but a witch hunt."

Dr. Thomas Radecki, of NCTV, told "60 Minutes" that the parents of a 17-year-old boy in Washington saw their son summon D&D "demons" moments before fatally shooting himself in the head. Radecki said another youth believed he would not be able to accomplish astral travel unless he shot himself.

The National Federation for Decency has long opposed Dungeons & Dragons. The *NFD Journal* quoted Dr. Gary North, author of "None Dare Call It Witchcraft" as follows, ". . . After years of study of the history of occultism . . . and after having consulted with scholars in the field of historical research, I can say with confidence: these games are the most effective, most magnificently packaged, most profitably marketed, most thoroughly researched introduction to the occult in man's recorded history."

The *NFD Journal* continued, "It is ludicrous to say that people, young or old, can immerse their minds and energies in violence, murder, human sacrifice, suicide, demonology, witchcraft, etc. without being intensely — and perhaps permanently — affected."

The crucial question remains: can Dungeons & Dragons or games of its kind actually be a factor in teenagers' decisions to commit suicide? The answer, no doubt, will continue to be debated in the months and years to come.

One person who answers in the affirmative is Dr. Charles Madsen Jr., a professor of psychology at Florida State University. He is a leading researcher on teenage suicides and was quoted by the *State Journal* in Frankfort, Ky.: "Internal pressures can come about through fantasy role playing. Kids with no strong sense of self-worth try to make up for it in fantasy games. They get overly involved. If there is an identity problem, if they feel they don't belong, the fantasy can become real, to the point it becomes part of them. If they are unhappy with themselves, they may have an overwhelming desire to change the situation, and suicide is a means of doing that."

Madsen said that most teenagers who commit suicide are not mentally ill. "Less than 10 percent have mental problems," he said. "All teenagers have problems, even the most well-adjusted can have stressful experiences that they feel they cannot deal with. As a general rule, individuals who attempt suicide do have problems, but not necessarily psychological or mental problems. If something is not done, we're on the verge of a teen suicide epidemic. There are currently ten attempts to every one that is successful."

Statistics show that there are an average of 5,000 teenage

suicides every year in the U.S.

B.A.D.D. lists 18 "early warning signs" of teenage suicide. They are 1) changes in eating and sleeping habits; 2) appearing edgy or somber, moody; 3) lack of interest in family activity; 4) lack of interest in things that previously pleased him or her, 5) withdrawal from family or friends; 6) persistent boredom; 7) decline in quality of school work; 8) radical personality change; 9) violent or rebellious behavior; 10) running away from home; 11) unusual neglect of appearance; 12) drug and alcohol abuse; 13) difficulty concentrating; 14) psychosomatic complaints; 15) teen telling parents he is unhappy or not loved; 16) teen telling parents he wants to die or kill himself; 17) total preoccupation with a fantasy role playing game; 18) walking about the house acting out the fantasy role-playing character.

8

Traditional Satanism

Whenever police investigators uncover evidence indicating the presence of worshippers of Satan, there is one book almost certain to be found. That volume is a 272-page paperback, published by the reputable New York firm of Avon Books, entitled *The Satanic Bible*.

Since its first appearance in December, 1969, *The Satanic Bible* has gone through 30 printings. Hundreds of thousands of copies of this volume have been sold around the country. The book sells steadily, year after year, and can be found in stock at almost any bookstore that carries paperback editions, including such national companies as Walden Books, B. Dalton Bookseller and many others.

Relatively little is known about The Church of Satan's founder, Anton Szandor LaVey, other than material issued by the church itself. Biographical information about LaVey is included in a ten-page introduction to *The Satanic Bible*, written by Burton H. Wolfe, an author whose previous works include such titles as *The Hippies, Hitler and the Nazis, The Devil and Dr. Moxin, Pileup on Death Row,* and *The Devil's Avenger.* The latter volume is a biography of LaVey, which Wolfe says was published in 1974 by Pyramid Books, a paperback publishing house.

According to author Wolfe, LaVey was born in 1930, The young LaVey, at the age of five, became fascinated by tales of the occult and supernatural published in the old *Weird Tales* pulp magazines. He also was a devotee of the classic novels, *Frankenstein* by Mary Shelley and Bram Stoker's *Dracula.*

At the age of 12, LaVey read lots of military manuals and decided that the Christian Bible was incorrect. He began to believe that the world would be inherited by the mighty, not the meek as the Scriptures promised.

No one ever contended that Anton LaVey was a stupid man. His high school days gave evidence of a budding prodigy, although Wolfe has reported that LaVey expended most of his intellectual energies on subjects outside those taught in high school, such as music, metaphysics and the occult. Then just 15, LaVey was a second oboist with the San Francisco Ballet Symphony Orchestra.

LaVey dropped out of high school in his junior year and went off to join the Clyde Beatty Circus. His role with the circus was one suitable for a person of his youth. He was given the duties of feeding and watering lions and tigers. LaVey apparently did well with these chores and the circus owner eventually appointed the youngster as an assistant trainer.

By the time LaVey turned 18, he left the Beatty organization and connected with a carnival. There he became a magician's assistant, he was taught the intricacies of hypnosis and continued his studies into the occult. As a part-time musician he often played the organ at the carnival during the week and then would play hymns during evangelists' tent shows on Sundays.

LaVey made note of the hypocrisy of men who would be

in the audiences of girlie shows during the week, lusting after the half-clad young women in those performances. And he would see these same men in attendance at the tent church services on Sundays. He says that it was during this period that he began to crystalize his views on religion that would eventually lead him to form The Church of Satan.

LaVey married in 1951, left the raucous world of carnival life, and attended City College of San Francisco, majoring in criminology. He then became a photographer for the police department in San Francisco. He told biographer Wolfe that his experiences as a photographer, taking pictures of crime victims, led him to "detest the sanctimonious attitude of people toward violence, always 'saying it's God's will.' "

He spent three years with the police department, then went back to playing the organ in nightclubs and theaters. In his spare time, he devoted himself to intensive studies of the black arts. He began to conduct classes on the subject and eventually a "Magic Circle" was created, meeting to perform various magical rituals which LaVey says he discovered or originated. Eventually he decided to form The Church of Satan. The day of its birth was April 30, 1966, which was Walpurgist Night, an important festival for those involved in magic and witchcraft. It signifies the climax of the spring Equinox.

LaVey proclaimed the "beginning of the Satanic era." A publication from the Church of Satan admits that the church's initial growth came from coverage in the mass media, including LaVey's conducting of the funeral for a member of the U.S. Navy who had been killed in San Francisco.

The Church of Satan claims to have between 10,000 and 20,000 adherents in the U.S. The church is focused in its Central Grotto (congregation) in San Francisco. There the church accepts or rejects all potential members and charters other grottos (its name for congregations) across the country. According to its publications, isolated individuals relate directly to the Central Grotto and power to regulate members is in the hands of the head of the church (LaVey).

The Church of Satan does not demand that its priests necessarily be adept in performing rituals, but notes that pastoral and organizational abilities are desirable. The Church of Satan confers the rank of priest on persons who achieve a measurable degree of esteem or proficiency and/or success. The church observes that one's level of membership within the church is commensurate with his/her position outside The Church of Satan.

Rituals for The Church of Satan may be conducted by a de facto priest. Such a priest can be a celebrant member who has demonstrated a working knowledge of the church's tenets and has the ability to conduct services. Such de facto priests must be authorized by the Central Grotto in San Francisco.

The church holds that anyone may conduct a ritual, but that a priest is required for group worship. Group worship is not a requirement for the church but is strongly encouraged as a major reinforcement of the faith and instillation of power.

The group lists these requirements for worship: "Worship in The Church of Satan is based on the belief that man needs ritual, dogma, fantasy and enchantment. Worship consists of magical rituals and there are three basic kinds: sexual rituals, to fulfill a desire; compassionate rituals, to help another; and destructive rituals, used for anger, annoyance or hate." Grottos often meet on Friday evenings for group rituals.

The equipment needed to worship in The Church of Satan varies with the type of ritual performed. Items likely to be included are robes of different colors, an altar, the symbol of Baphomet (Satan), candles, a bell, a chalice, elixer (wine or some other drink pleasing to the palate), a sword, a model phallus, a gong and parchment paper. The church suggests that facilities for worship should be in a private place where an altar can be erected and rituals performed.

The Church of Satan has no dietary laws or restrictions on the diet of its adherents. The most important holiday for a member is his or her own birthday. The church's literature observes that "every man is a god as he chooses to recognize that fact." Other than one's birthday, other important dates for members of The Church of Satan include Walpurgis Night, the climax of the spring Equinox which also was the birthdate of the church itself and all hallow's eve. The Church of Satan also recommends celebrating the solstices and Equinoxes which occur in March, June, September and December and mark the first day of the new seasons.

The Church of Satan says that priests may perform funerals, but adds that the Central Grotto should be contacted in case of death. There is no prohibition on autopsies, but the church asks that cremations be permitted only in extreme circumstances, such as when it might be necessary to safeguard the health of others.

There are no restrictions on medical treatment and no dress code or uniform required. The church takes no position on serving in the armed forces. A priest is not required at the time of death.

According to The Church of Satan, its basic teachings or beliefs include the fact that it worships Satan, "most clearly symbolized in the Roman God Lucifer, the bearer of light, the spirit of the air, and the personification of enlightenment. The church claims not to visualize Satan as an anthropomorphic being. Rather Satan is seen to represent the forces of nature. Satanists, the church holds, see the self as the highest embodiment of human life. The self is sacred. LeVey claims that the Church of Satan is essentially a human potential movement. Its members are encouraged to develop whatever capabilities they can by which they might excel. But LaVey cautions that members should realize their limitations, which he calls an important factor in this philosophy of rational self-interest. The church asserts that its members practice "magick," which it defines as the art of changing situations or events in accordance with one's will, which would, using normally accepted methods, be impossible.

The accepted literature to provide direction for Satanists, The Church of Satan says, are three publications from the writings of LaVey: *The Satanic Bible, The Compleat Witch* and *The Satanic Rituals*. But members are also "encouraged" to study what are called "pertinent" writings which serve as guidelines for Satanic thought, such as works of Mark Twain, Machiavelli, George Bernard Shaw, Ayn Rand and Fredrich Nietzsche, as well as others who espouse anti-Christian theology.

Beyond the nine Satanic statements which are published in *The Satanic Bible*, LaVey says that the church generally opposes the use of narcotics which dull the senses. He also condemns suicide and says that he stands firmly for law and order, stating that The Church of Satan "is not to be confused with 'Satanist' groups which have been found to engage in illegal acts."

The Church of Satan says that it does not actively seek out new members, but that it welcomes inquiries from "honest potential Satanists who hear about the church from the various books about it, the mass media or word-of-mouth." The claim is made that the church screens potential new members before they are accepted.

Persons who write to The Church of Satan's headquarters in San Francisco (the church uses a post office box to receive inquiries) will receive a form letter. That letter states:

"As an elitist organization, The Church of Satan grants Active Membership to only those individuals who meet its requirements. If you are sincerely interested in affiliation with us, or simply credit The Church of Satan with establishing the world's most formidable threat to hypocrisy, the first step is simple.

"We make no false claims of altruism; we realize what we

have, what we are, and what we shall become. Knowing relatively little of you, we accept your professed interest or dedication at face value. We have every desire to incorporate valid members into our plans for the future, so we suggest that you become a Contributing Member.

"For $50.00 you will receive an identification card, an amulet bearing the symbol of The Church of Satan, your first year's subscription to our publication: The Cloven Hoof, and information on how to progress more deeply into Satanism — its philosophy, rituals, locations, means of meeting other Satanists, and sources of supply for working materials unique to Satanic magic. You will also receive a questionnaire, should you wish to apply for Active Membership status.

"Our scope is unlimited, and the extent and degree of your involvement is based upon your own potential. All names and addresses are held confidential and you are under no further obligation as a Contributing Member, unless you desire otherwise."

MICHAEL AQUINO AND THE TEMPLE OF SET

Another group of interest in any discussion of The Church of Satan is the Temple of Set, which was founded by Michael A. Aquino, an Army Reserve lieutenant colonel who lives in California.

Aquino became affiliated with The Church of Satan and Anton LaVey in 1969, then broke away from LaVey in 1975. Then he formed the Temple of Set, which he describes as a non-profit church incorporated in the state of California and recognized by state and federal tax agencies.

Set is defined by Aquino as another name for Satan, coming from the hieroglyphic Set-hen, the god's formal title. Literature from the Temple of Set says that the devil was "an object of fear to dogmatists and theologians, but to free and creative spirits he became a symbol of human pride and genius. The savagery directed against medieval and Renaissance Satanists resulted in the recorded deaths by torture of numerous Europeans. So effective was this persecution that Satanists could not surface openly until 1966 (when The Church of Satan was formed). The present Temple of Set restores the essence of its ancient forerunner — and adds to it 2,000 years' experience along the Left-Hand Path."

Functions and services of the Temple of Set are called deliberately individualistic. "There are no congregations of docile 'followers' — only cooperative philosophers and magicians. Through correspondence and personal contact, however, many Setians develop close friendships, as well as stimulating intellectual and magical contacts for both brief and extensive research projects and ritual workings."

Aquino has been described by a former member of the Temple of Set as "a proficient propagandist, political scientist, and psychological warfare expert."

Aquino's writings are couched in somewhat difficult-to-follow intellectual mumbo-jumbo, making them hard to comprehend. Formal followers of the Temple of Set are few in number; even Aquino himiself admits that. In 1985, he wrote in a letter that "during its lifetime the Temple of Set's membership has ranged from 50 to 150 at any one time, of whom virtually all are seriously interested. The satisfying of this interest for so many unique individuals is a very demanding task, hence the Temple already has far more to do than we have time and resources available. Far from wanting to expand rapidly, we want to grow very slowly—so that we can ensure that those who do enter receive the degree of attention, assistance and services a Setian should be able to expect."

Interestingly, Aquino claims in this letter that The Church of Satan's membership ranged from only 200 to 350 people at any one time, "of whom perhaps 25 were more than casually interested 'subscribers.' " This number is in stark contrast to The Church of Satan's claims of 10,000 to 20,000 members. However, it must be realized that the great preponderance of the followers of The Church of Satan have never formally made an effort to actually "join" the church. The thousands who follow portions of the teachings of Anton LaVey and others of his like are not those who send in their $50 payments to become contributing members. The majority of the followers of the precepts of The Church of Satan are those teenagers who pay the $3.95 purchase price for a copy of the paperback edition of *The Satanic Bible*. And it seems that many of those who read the writings of LaVey choose to overlook the author's cautions against breaking the law, etc.

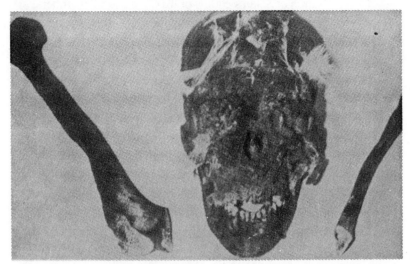

Skull caked with dirt, rust, and chicken feathers. Portions of long bones have been sawed off. The presence of rust, dirt, and chicken feathers leaves no doubt that these were used for rituals of Santeria.

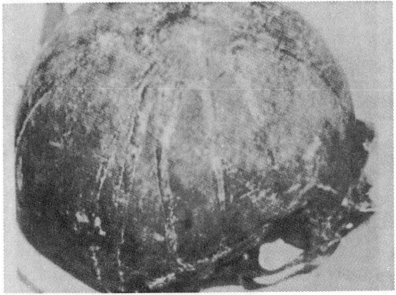

Skull with adherent streams of wax and the imprint of a candle on top skull. Taken from *Forensic Sciences Aspects of Santeria A religious cult of African origin*, by C. V. Wetli, MD and R. Martinez, MA.

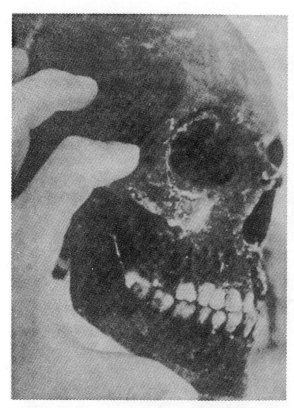

Skull found in shallow grave. Used for the rites of Santeria. Taken from *Forensic Sciences Aspects of Santeria, A religious cult of African origin,* by C.V. Wetli, MD and R. Martinez, MA.

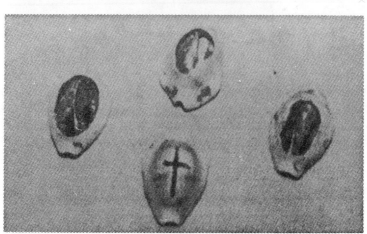

Cowrie shells found with the nganga.

Eleggua
(one of the
seven
African
powers).

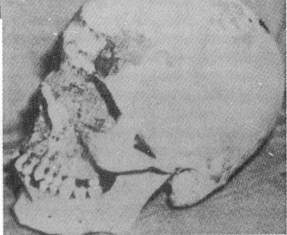

Skull with cowrie shell found on railroad tracks.

A Nganga complete with skull, railroad spikes, and glyphs as well as symbolism of Santeria.

Taken from *Brujeria-Manifestations of Palo Mayomba in South Florida*, by Charles V. Wetli, MD and Rafael Marinez, MA.

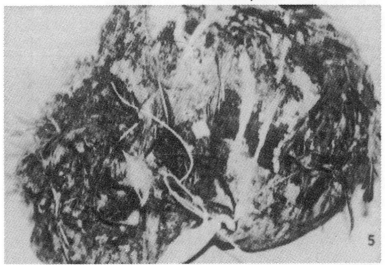

Skull found in a Nganga and covered with feathers, wax, and blood.

Copyright-ASTM 1916 Race Street, Philadelphia, PA 19103. Reprinted from *J. Forensic Science 26:506-514, 1981*, with permission.

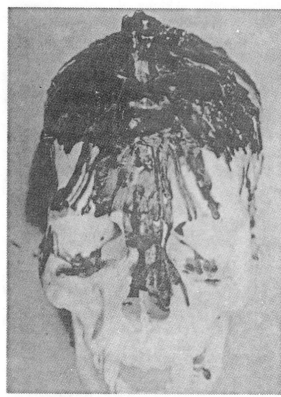

Skull with streams of wax and a black candle. Using a human skull is very common among the Santeria.

Skull with adherent blood, feathers, and wax found in a cemetery with items from a dismantled Nganga. Taken from *Brujeria manifestations of Palo Mayombe in South Florida*, by Charles V. Wetli, MD and Rafael Martinez, MA.

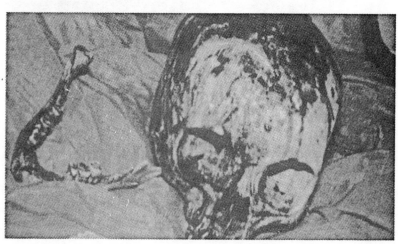

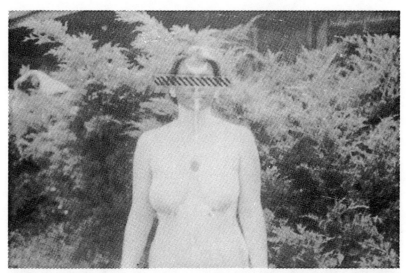

TOP. Body language is used for ritual purposes also. The signs and symbols used all have meaning. The back of this person has purification symbols painted on her back. BOTTOM. Purification plays a very important part of the ritual. In fact at this gathering they had a sweat lodge that they would go into and cleanse themselves before worshipping their dieties. (Paganism)

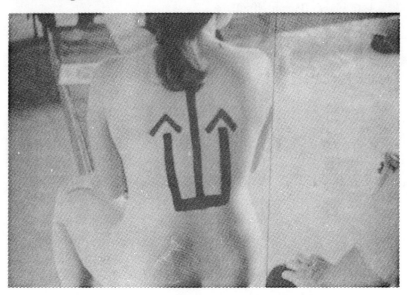

Tom Wedge photographed this group of witches representing different covens or groups from across the eastern part of the United States as the procession began to come in to form the circle around the altar and fire. A large chalice was passed around the circle and each person drank from the chalice. He was told that this was a very sacred item and it is kept in a safe place. (Pagan ritual)

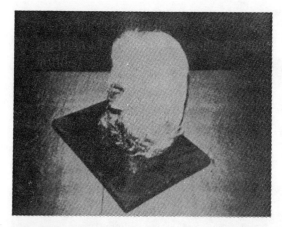

Sympathetic magic can be practiced in many ways. A practitioner can make a human head to represent the person who has offended them. This is used in the same manner voodoo dolls are used. They can be made from paper, wood, straw, wax, cloth or those dolls sold at retail stores.

This decomposed head is also used in sympathetic magic. This figure becomes the person that the practitioner is trying to harm through a hex or a spell.

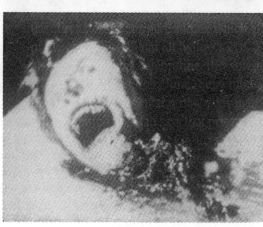

Again, sympathetic magic. The images represent a person who has offended the practitioner. The head is used the same as a voodoo doll would be used. If possible the practitioner will try to get something personal from the person they are casting the spell upon. It can be hair, nail clippings, clothing, photos, anything. They will go through a very complex ritual that can last several days.

135

This hand is used in sympathetic magic. The hand becomes the hand of the person who had offended the practitioner. The practitioner is using the hand just as one would use a voodoo doll to cause harm to the enemy who has offended them.

Practitioners of both white and black magic can buy any type of occult items needed to practice their magic from mail order occult stores or warehouses. This photo shows many different types of candles that the practitioner can purchase to use. Very few will make their own anymore. It's much easier to just order them in any color they want, and for any rituals as well.

9

Non-Traditional Satanism and Evidence of Satanic Worship Today

C.A.S.H. (Continental Association of Satan's Hope)

As an example of the slickly written and powerfully enticing messages expounded by those who claim to follow Satan, I offer you some of the diabolical writings of a group based in Montreal, Canada. C.A.S.H., which stands for the Continental Association of Satan's Hope, sends out a four-page brochure which promises fame and fortune through its book, *The Magic Power of Satan*. The volume is offered for $23 through the mail, with the notation that checks be made out to CASH (isn't that a clever one!)

Part of the text of this brochure follows:

"The mighty power of our lord Satan can now become part of you! Whatever you need or want, our lord Satan can get it for you quickly and easily! You can now discover for yourself a new world through the infernal power of the mighty Satan, lord and rightful ruler of this earth! Find out how you too can realize your lifelong ambitions once you pledge allegiance to the true king of this world! It does not matter what your goals are, whether you want infinite wealth, or just a comfortable new home, fine possessions, love, companionship, new health and vigour, power over others, our lord Satan can bring it to you! You will be absolutely amazed how lifelong obstacles will disappear, and life will become such a pleasure to live, once our lord Lucifer becomes a part of your life!"

The brochure goes on to ridicule Christianity, stating that "The church knows only too well that once you discover the true and rightful ruler of this world, and learn to draw from our master's fantastic sea of power they will most definitely lose you as a follower as well as placing their very purpose for existing in a certain suicidal positon. After all, who is going to follow someone who says that happiness is weakness, suffering, shortage of money, when you can become strong and powerful and able to fulfill your desires and enjoy life instead of suffering through it. That's right, who is going to go to church to grovel or pray on Sunday and give continual donations in the hope that they will eventually become happy — although they never do become so."

C.A.S.H. says that Satanic magic brings automatic success and cures illness.

Even more enticing to young people, whose self-esteem is battered and weak, is this group's promise to reveal the "secrets of persuasion." The brochure asks the question, "do you know that you can get someone to do your bidding, to accept your commands, to do as you order? Through the power of our lord Satan you can implant thoughts in other people's minds! You can use Satanic power to dominate others! Control your boss where you work! Make someone love you! Attract women! Attract men! Leave your enemies wishing they were your friends! People will act toward you how you want! Best of all, no one will ever suspect that they are under your power!"

If there is any doubt about the increase in Satanic worship in the present time, it might serve to look over some of the hundreds of stories that have been printed in the nation's press over the past few years. Although some students of modern-day Satanism have objected to how Satan and his followers have been written about in the public press, in most cases newspapers and magazines have relied upon police and court documents as well as independent investigative reporting in publishing a tremendous amount of information about the increasing problem of Satanic cults today.

In September, 1985 the *Associated Press* reported that symbols of devil worship were found in the homes of some of the victims of the "Night Stalker," who is believed responsible for 16 slayings. The story from Los Angeles added that the prime suspect, Richard Ramirez, was obsessed with a heavy-metal song about a "Night Prowler."

Ramirez was arrested in East Los Angeles after he was chased down and beaten by a group of residents when he allegedly punched a woman and tried to steal a car.

Police told the AP that Ramirez was the principal suspect in a series of 14 slayings and dozens of other felonies that occurred between Feb. 8, 1985 and the time of his arrest. Victims were shot, bludgeoned, stabbed or had their throats slashed by an assailant who sneaked into darkened homes through unlocked doors or windows. Unidentified sources told the *Los Angeles Times* and Los Angeles television stations KABC and KCBS that pentagrams were painted on walls in the homes of some of the Night Stalker's victims. KABC said that the killer tried to gouge out an eye of at least one victim and ate meals in some victims' homes. The wife of one victim testified later that Ramirez forced her to "swear on Satan" she wouldn't alert neighbors by screaming.

Ray Garcia, identified as a former classmate of Ramirez, told the San Francisco Examiner that Ramirez was obsessed with Satanic themes in the rock band AC-DC's 1979 album,

"Highway to Hell." The album cover shows a band member dressed as a devil, while another musician wears a pentagram-shaped pendant. Garcia also said that Ramirez' favorite song was "Night Prowler."

Later, when Ramirez appeared in a Los Angeles courtroom, he raised his right hand, his palm displaying an inked pentagram.

Three recent cases from Virginia are further evidence of the outbreak of Satanism.

The Christian Inquirer published a report about vandalism at four churches in Norfolk, Va., over a two-month period. Workers arriving at the Temple Baptist Church found Satanic slogans and symbols written across the building in indelible ink.

The Rev. Mark Pullen said someone had written the words "Burn in hell" and "Satan rules" in four-inch letters across the front doors of the church. An inverted cross, a Satanic symbol, and "666" were drawn on the cement pavement in front of the church.

In Portsmouth, Va., vandals broke into the home of Lauralee W. Martini, in the middle of the day where they smashed crystal and cut telephone lines. They sprayed mace in one room and twisted and burned the eyeglasses of her 10-year-old child. No members of the family were home at the time of the entry.

Mrs. Martini told the Virginian Pilot newspaper that the attacker pulled out the feathers of their parrot Eric, then pulled off the parrot's head and used its bloodied body to make marks and crosses and to write "666" on the walls. She said the vandals tried to mount the head of the parrot on a candle.

In Williamsburg, Va., the *Daily Press of Newport News* reported that a man was charged with burglary after he allegedly entered the Williamsburg United Methodist Church and set up a devil worship display in the sanctuary. The Rev. David H. Smith, pastor of the church, said when he arrived early in the morning at the church he found an array of six red candles in a circle before the communion rail, centered by a large white candle. "I found an insignia hanging from the altar and an inverted cross," as well as an American flag.

When police arrived at the church, they found a 20-year-old man asleep in the church balcony. The man told authorities that he was a Satan worshipper.

In Houston, Texas, five teenagers who claimed to believe in Satanism were arrested and accused of luring a 19-year-old laborer to a field behind a cemetery where they tortured him and then killed him because "they wanted to watch somebody die."

Sheriff's Detective Max Cox of Harris County, Texas, told the *Boston Chronicle* that "they sat around and talked about it for a week and then lured him out to the field and killed him for kicks."

In Monroe, Mich., the shotgun slaying of a teenager by his younger brother was "the acting out of a Satanic sacrifice," sheriff's investigators told the *Detroit Free Press*. Chief investigator Lt. Michael Davison said officers had uncovered groups at three Monroe County high schools involved in Satan worship. He said the groups were small — perhaps involving no more than "roughly a dozen" students in total — and that the killing was not part of any group activity.

The superintendent of the school attended by the teenager accused of killing his brother said high school officials had removed "three or four drawings relating to Satanic worship" from school walls. One, depicting a fiery, goat-headed devil being crucified, was found posted in a boys restroom.

Davison told a news conference that the date of the killing — Feb. 2, 1986 — was significant because it was a "witches' sabbath." Items seized by investigators and displayed at the news conference included a black hooded robe, a dagger, a machete, a black candle, inverted cross medallions, books on Satanic rituals and rock music tapes by heavy metal

141

performers including Ozzy Osbourne, Black Sabbath and KISS.

Davison said he believed the teenagers' involvement in Satanic worship is more than adolescent dabbling. "We believe they are serious about what they are doing," he said.

In April of 1986, the *Albuquerque (N.M.) Journal* published a story about the police search for a 15-year-old boy who was sought in connection with shooting his father to death with a bow and arrow. The youngster allegedly had vowed to get revenge on his father for tearing up the youth's Satanic Bible.

An affidavit filed in court said police found Satanic symbols in the youth's bedroom. His parents were divorced and he lived with his father. The youth's mother told authorities that the boy had called her two weeks prior to the murder, saying that he was very upset because his father had ripped in half a copy of *The Satanic Bible*. The youngster told his mother that he would "get even" with his father. Police found a Satanic symbol, a star with the number 666 inside, drawn on the carpet in red. An identical symbol was drawn on the closet door and below it was written "Satan Rules."

Scripps Howard News Service, whose reports are published in newspapers across the U.S., reported in September 1986 that "as many as 800 crimes now under investigation by police nationwide are said to be linked somehow to devil worship."

The story said scores of reports link child molestation to Satanic rituals featuring chalices of blood and participants either nude or wearing black hoods.

Roger Burt, an evangelical minister and president of the Christian Counseling Association in Los Angeles, believes that the current outbreak of Satanism is part of a lengthy war between the forces of good and evil. Burt said the people who are getting involved in Satanism are looking to get the power of demons and use it for themselves. "It all centers on power over their peers, especially among teenagers, which is where this is growing fastest," he said. "This is not just a fad of the '80s. It is actual spiritual warfare. Spiritual possession has great power in attracting young people."

Evangelist Jack Van Impe of Royal Oak, Mich. has preached and written about Satanic worship and the world of the occult. He says that his 1985 publication, "Exorcism and the Spirit World," was written to prove "the reality and power of Satan and his emissaries and (to warn Christians) of the danger inherent in associating with any form of the occult."

Van Impe has written that "Satan is powerful, but he does not possess the attributes of God Almighty. Satan is mighty, but not almighty. He is intelligent, but not omniscient or all-knowing. God Almighty knows everything, whereas Satan is limited in knowledge. Satan is not omnipresent — everywhere at once — as God the Father is. God alone is omniscient and omnipresent.

The Michigan evangelist has received numerous letters from prison inmates who have commented on their experiences with the Devil and the occult.

One letter, from a 40-year-old woman on Death Row in Florida, states that she had been "a Satanist from age 23 with the occult 'Masters of Lucifer,' Before that from 14 to 23, I belonged to an occult 'Teens of Lucifer,' And before that from 5 to 14, I had been kicked from one foster home to another. ... So I was an easy prey for Satan. In my thirteenth year, I was sent to a girls welfare home because I ran away from the home of my father. There I met teens who were 'Children of Lucifer.' And they had everything — money, nice clothing, outside jobs, and lots more. I was told if I became a member, I, too, would receive from Father Lucifer all my heart's desires. So I joined and for 26 years no Christian materials ever passed through my hands. One year ago I was tried and convicted of a death that had happened 15 years before. I was given the death penalty and am now on Florida's death row. Satan is a busy fellow — he never gives up. If he wants this clay body, fine, take it — but praise God, my spirit belongs to my Creator and I will spend eternity in the presence of God, my Father, and Jesus Christ my saviour."

Another letter to Van Impe came from a convict in Jefferson City, Mo., who wrote that he had studied and practiced witchcraft and Satanism for many years, along with Eastern philosophies of all kinds. "I know the devastating effect it has on a person over a period of time," this man wrote. "I am serving a natural/life sentence as a result of not knowing the dangers of Satanism and eventually not caring. I pray that someday I can talk to one person and be able to fully explain to that person the living hell he's setting himself up for when he messes with the occult. And if my talking to him will change his mind and turn him away from Satanism or witchcraft or whatever guise it's hiding under, then I can know that I have literally saved that person's life. If so doing, maybe I can make amends in the only way I know how for the life I took. . ."

10

Crime Scene Investigations

Of interest to the general reader as well as law enforcement officers is the following list of some of the things officials may come across during crime scene investigations:

1. Mockery of Christian symbols, such as an inverted cross.

2. Discovery of candles or candle drippings of different colors.

3. Non-discernible alphabets.

4. Unusual drawings or symbols on walls or coverings, such as pentagrams, hexagrams, etc.

5. Use of stolen or vandalized Christian artifacts.

6. Use of animal parts (feathers, hair, bones) to form signs and symbols on the ground as well as human body parts.

7. Investigators should look for the absence of blood in an animal.

8. Officers should work closely with humane societies to assure that autopsies are performed on animal carcasses that may be found. Autopsies cannot only determine if an animal

has had its blood removed, but also often can ascertain the cause of death, such as electrocution.

9. Animal mutilations, as well as human mutilations including the removal of specific body parts, such as the anus, heart, tongue, ears. For instance, Satan worshippers might remove a dog's front legs, as they believe that Satan can use the legs to move around.

10. Effigies, such as voodoo dolls stuck with pins. Such dolls are often made out of straw, or wax, or even paper. Others are constructed from cloth. Some are manufactured items purchased in stores. The method used does not matter.

11. Investigators should look for altars containing artifacts, such as chalices, parts of human skulls, athame, candles of different colors signifying different types of rituals. The altar can be located in a small area, such as a closet or in a small corner of a room. The altar room usually is painted black, other times, it will consist of red walls with a black ceiling. Windows usually are covered so that no light shines in.

12. Bowls, in the form of sea shells, or regular bowls made from wood, glass or human skulls. The bowls may contain different colored powders, which may be made from dried wolf's eyes or dried bat's blood.

13. A skull, with or without candles. A skull can be that of a human or it can be a simulated human skull. At occult stores, a real human skull may sell for as much as $150. Skulls manufactured from fiberglass or other materials may sell for $50 or less.

14. Robes, especially black, light or scarlet.

15. Rooms that are draped in black or red materials.

16. Books about Satanism, which play an important part in rituals.

17. Candle drippings, the colors of which will indicate the type of ceremony conducted at the scene. (See next chapter.)

18. Statues, which are used to protect ritual areas from demonic forces.

For homicide investigations, I tell those in my seminars that officers should treat any occult scene as one would any homicide scene. I advise that officers investigate from the outside perimeter in. I tell them to take as many photographs as possible, carefully photographing and diagramming the position of the body.

Officers should locate the stab wounds and cuts, noting any missing body parts. For instance, if a body's right hand is tied or taped down, their chest has been cut open and heart taken, this is a definite indication of Satanic involvement. Tying or taping down the right hand shows that an effort has been made to deny Jesus Christ, who sits at the right hand of the Father. One's right hand indicates righteousness. Since the heart represents the center of life among Satanists, then removal of the heart and the right hand tied down would certainly indicate that the murder was related to Satanism.

As far as stab wounds and cuts go, in most cult-related cases, stab wounds will not be of a penetrating nature. Usually the wounds will be found around the neck area, the intention being to render the victim unconscious. Other wounds will be inflicted later, after any mutilation takes place.

I suggest that investigators look for evidence of wax drippings either on the body or in the immediate vicinity. I ask them to note the color of any drippings that they might find, as the color cast sheds a tremendous amount of information about the case.

I advise that officers look for branding or burn marks on the victim. Officers also are urged to determine if incense or oils have been used, which is quite common with occult-related killings.

Investigators might want to determine if the victim had been used in a sex ritual. Check for evidence of sperm both on the victim's clothing and body. If a sex ritual occurred, there may not have been intercourse with the victim, but a cult member may have ejaculated on the victim's clothes or body itself.

It's a good idea to watch for any trace of animal or human feces on the victim.

Another recommendation is to have the victim's stomach analyzed for any evidence of urine, blood or drugs that could have been used to make the victim lose consciousness and then be offered as a sacrifice.

In investigating, it is important not only to carefully look at everything on the ground or floor level, but to look over the area above as well. I suggest that officers check trees for strings, ribbons and marking spots. They should look beyond the actual location, as the sacrifice might be in one area and then the victim could have been transported to another area to continue the ritual.

I cannot overemphasize how important it is that investigators note the position of the body, be it human or animal. Make detailed drawings of the body's position, noting the directions (north, south, etc.).

SIGNS AND SYMBOLS

If a pentagram star is turned so that only one point is on top, this is a sign of white magic. The top point represents the spirit and the others stand for wind, fire, earth and water.

A hexagram is basically the Seal of Solomon, not to be confused with the Star of David. It is one of the most powerful symbols in the occult.

Trail markers are distinguishing lines that give directions to the places various occult groups practice their beliefs. The markers serve as maps, giving information on how to reach the practice sites. There are different types of markers; each can be unique and apply only to one particular group. One symbol, a double-bladed axe in an upright position, represents anti-justice. It also can represent death.

148

A triangle may vary in size, but generally is drawn on the ground. It is a place where a demon may appear if conjured up during a ritual ceremony.

A talisman or amulet is an object which in drawing or writing inscribes a god's name or image of a supernatural power that protects the wearer of the object.

A circle has different meanings. One is eternity, since a circle has no ending. Another is as a protection from evil. Often you will find a circle and inside it will be an inverted pentagram. It can be made from string, sand, lime and even from the imagination. But a circle cannot have a break anywhere, since it serves as a protection against evil forces that are conjured up during incantations. In some cases, a circle is nine feet in diameter. This is not always required, however, as circles can be of any size.

Different symbols often are found during criminal investigations. Some are carved on human victims, usually when the victim has betrayed the group, has become a traitor in some respect as far as others in the group are concerned.

An inverted cross of Satanic justice is an upside-down cross. It has a small half-circle on the cross member. The very tips are bent. The center vertical line indicates a man's presence. The horizontal line indicates eternity, past and future. The arc indicates the world. The inverted cross symbolizes the utopia of anti-Christian theology.

The sexual ritual symbol is used to indicate the place and purpose. It is often carved into stone, or painted on the sign of a road, to show present use of that particular location. A blood ritual symbol represents human and animal sacrifices. It is a half-moon and contains other symbols.

There are two styles of black mass indicators.

The astrological symbols include a circle containing a dot, which represents Sol, which is Sunday. Then there is the crescent moon in reverse, or Luna, which is Monday. The symbol for Mars represents Tuesday, Mercury signifies

Wednesday, Jupiter stands for Thursday. Venus stands for Friday and Saturn represents Saturday.

All these symbols can be utilized in Satanic worship.

TYPES OF WRITING USED IN THE OCCULT

There are many types of writing used in the occult. Each has its own characteristics. Satanists sometimes use part, all or just one. First is the Runes alphabet, which was almost completely destroyed. Much of it was handed down through the ages by memory. Then there is the Theban alphabet, also known as the Witches alphabet or Satanic alphabet. Next is the Hebrew alphabet, which often is used.

Also used are Malachim writings, Pafsings, and others.

11

Candles

Anna Riva is author of a book, *Candleburning Magic*. She states in that volume: "The rules are few and easy to follow. All that's required for success is a candle, a purpose and a concentrated force of power directed toward the objective through one's mental energies. Any kind of candles can be used. You can make them yourself or buy them, but they must be new and used for one purpose only. The size and shape is not indicative of the success of the rites. Once used in a ritual, a candle should not be used again for a new or different intentions even if the candle is only partially consumed. A candle can be lighted, allowed to burn for a period of time, the flame extinguished and then relighted again and again, hourly, daily or weekly, whatever schedule you have decided upon. But if your purpose changes, start with new candles each time."

There are more than 200 books that have been published on the subject of candle colors. In this volume, I will cover only those colors that are of great value, as far as practitioners are concerned.

Black candles are used for evil, loss, adversity, protection from evil spirits, as a shield from the evil eye, and to repel black magic.

Blue candles represent truth, health, inspiration, wisdom, immortality, royalty, sincerity, devotion, kindness, patience, fidelity, honesty, peace and harmony in the home.

Brown candles signify a balance, a concentration, indecision, telepathic power, study, initiative, communication, earthiness, thrift.

Green stands for abundance, cooperation, generosity, fertility, success, luck, money, ambition, greed, envy, peace, harmony, health and healing.

Orange represents joy, enthusiasm, friendship, attraction, stimulation, self-control, adaptability, intellect and organization.

Pink stands for affection, service, love, honor, spiritual awakening, unselfishness, leadership, and it represents the feminine part of a person.

Purple involves dignity, ambition, idealism, wisdom, psychic ability, power, progress, independence, protection, pride and honor.

Red stands for life, love, sex, courage, energy, strength, health, impulsive fiery willpower, conceit, vitality and magnetism.

White signifies purity, truth, sincerity, spirtuality, wholeness, generosity, expansion, outgoing cleansing, respect, innocence, prophecy and clairvoyance.

Yellow represents unity, success, universal love, activity, creativity, action. It can be used to develop occult powers, invoke spirits, for inspiration and concentration.

Next, let's look at image candles, in which different images are used for different purposes.

The wax cat candle comes in many different colors and

can be used for a number of purposes, depending on the color. For instance, red cat candles can be used for love objectives, by annointing them with an oil and burning them when the loved one is present.

Cross or crucifix candles are shaped as a cross. Some of them are upside down, which indicates blasphemy for what the cross stands for (the crucifixion of Christ)..Some candles will depict a serpent (representing Satan) wrapped around the cross, again indicating blasphemy.

The Satan candle is used in black magic and for hexes, curses and the like. The candle is annointed with what is termed a devil's oil or crossing oil. It is burned for an hour, beginning at midnight, and this continues each night until the mission is accomplished. When the candle is lighted, a chant is employed to call or summon demonic forces that are sought to carry out evil deeds. In addition, the curse or message is written on a piece of parchment and usually is set down in some form of blood, either dragon's or bat's. The parchment is then burned in the flame of the candle as a certain chant is said.

The figure or image candles also come in different colors. Figure candles are used in the same manner as would be a voodoo doll. They can be using in hexing, for passion. Image candles can represent either men or women.

Another candle, shaped in the form of a mummy case, is called a mummy candle. This particular kind of candle is a rare and unique candle, used primarily for spells seeking power and success. It is annointed with mummy oil and placed on an altar with a burner filled with powerful incense. The incense burns for 10 to 15 minutes while the Satanists concentrate on the project at hand. Then the candle itself is lit and the chant is repeated for several minutes.

Next are reversible candles, which are basically red in color but the outer surface has been dipped in black. Thus, when lighted, the dark, harmful elements are first burned away, exposing the bright, energizing vibrations which emit from the red center. Usually the candle is dressed with reversible oil and burned for an hour each day until the negative force which has enveloped the person has been broken. The powers of light and energy then can spread those soothing and enlightened rays through their lives.

A wishing candle, also called the seven-knob candle, looks like seven balls, stacked atop each other. These candles come in different colors. Each ball is burned, perhaps with a message attached to each ball, over a period of seven days. At the end of that period, the particular hex or whatever is then complete.

Skull candles, which also come in several colors, are used primarily for hexing and separating purposes. The white version of this candle is used to help someone who is ill recover from that illness. Green skull candles are used to separate a person from his money. A red skull candle can be burned to cause love between two people to die. The red version also can be utilized to cause a person to move from their home. Black skulls are used with care, since this candle — the Satanists believe — can cause severe suffering and pain. Those who use forces affected by the black candle lightly and without cause may have those forces come back on the user.

The snake candle is used for protection from evil. These candles are usually large, about two inches in diameter and eight to nine inches in length. A thin, waxen snake is superimposed around the candle, with the snake's tail at the bottom and mouth at the top. The purpose of this candle is to acknowledge that there are light and dark forces in all things and that evil influences must be negated and thrust away before the good can blossom and take over. The candles are anointed with protection oil and used once each month to keep the home free from harm.

The witch candles, constructed in the shape of a witch, are used for love spells.

Candles play a very important role in rituals. In many cases, detection of drippings, and especially the colors used, can be extremely helpful to an investigator in determining what occurred at the site. Many times, such evidence is overlooked. These types of candles are not normally found on display in the average home.

For example, in a murder case I was called in to look at the crime scene. What I found was several black candles that had been burnt. After careful examination, I noticed a golden type item embedded in one of the spent candles. This was a button of a person that was being hexed. This particular practitioner kept the spent candles to make figure candles out of them to work sympathetic magic. The point is that you can make your investigation very easy if you know what you are looking for.

12

Santeria

Santeria is a religion with roots along the Niger River in Africa, with the Yoruba tribe, which spread to the Carribbean via Cuba on slave ships centuries ago. There it blended with Catholicism practiced by the Spanish overlords. Then, with the influx of Cuban refugees into the United States because of the political machinations of Fidel Castro, the Santeria cult has become prevalent wherever those of Cuban roots now reside in the U.S.

Santeria has been called a practical religion. Its believers beg favors from patron saints with chants and candles and, sometimes, animal sacrifices.

The *Los Angeles Times* reported that two young brothers found cauldrons in a Miami alleyway. The youngsters discovered all sorts of things packed inside, including candles, horseshoes, magnets, shells and a woman's skull. Dr. Charles V. Wetli, deputy chief medical examiner for the Miami-Dade County area, knew what it was all about.

"Magic," he said, after sorting through five cauldrons that contained railroad spikes, mousetraps, toy guns, a lawn mower blade, turtle heads and a dried toad. Wetli said the "magic" in Miami includes drum ceremonies in the night, slaughtered animals floating down the Miami River and an apple impaled on a cross outside a judge's chambers.

Some Cubans living in Miami not only practice Santeria, but also indulge in Palo Mayombe, a black magic sect of Santeria which has roots in the Congo. Its priests, called paleros, perform rituals to communicate with the dead. For such ceremonies, they fill cauldrons with sacred dirt, trinkets, animal parts and human bones.

Wetli said the cauldrons found by the Miami youths were part of Palo Mayombe, the more malevolent cult. Another case occurring about the same time came to Wetli's attention. When a man was arrested, a skull fell from underneath his T-shirt as he tried to flee. When he was apprehended, he possessed a dead turtle and a bag filled with human hair.

Wetli has become a student of Santeria and Palo through his perspective as a medical examiner. He says that Palo Mayombe is "primarily involved in malevolent sorcery. It's black magic, to inflict harm."

Wetli and Rafael Martinez are co-authors of several articles about the two religions. One paper, "Santeria: A Magico-Religious System of Afro-Cuban Origin," was presented in 1981 to the American Association for Social Psychiatry in New York.

The two men say that increased evidence of Santeria can be a "functional strategy of conflict resolution, both at the individual and the interpersonal levels." Wetli and Martinez write, "The system provides an outlet for repressed hostilities."

When Negro slaves were first brought to the New World, in many instances they were forbidden to continue to practice the religions of their native countries. Their owners and overseers demanded that the slaves be introduced to

Christianity. The result was an amalgam of religions, with bits of the African religions being merged into those taught by their Christian owners. Santeria became a religion that involved worship of facimilies of Roman Catholic saints. In fact, the word Santeria literally means "saint worship."

The African gods and goddesses of Santeria are of West African origin, according to Wetli and Martinez. Specifically these gods come from the Yoruba culture of southwestern Nigeria. The resulting religion of Santeria sees various gods or goddesses as having unique powers and a specific domain.

Each believer, according to the tenents of Santeria, is born with a particular guardian santo (saint) that must be worshipped throughout life. Whether the believer performs a simple ritual of thanksgiving or goes through an elaborate initiation ritual to become a santero (priest), the guardian santo is central to all of the ritual offerings, incantations, magic and spirit possession states characteristic of Santeria rituals.

Rituals extensively utilize roots, herbs, flowers and plants. More than 500 different herbs have been given attributes of various medicinal and/or magical properties. Most of the religious items can be purchased from stores called botanicas, Such stores are located throughout the Miami area, for instance, and supply a variety of ritualistic paraphernalia.

Most formal Santeria rituals also require the use of sacrificial birds and animals. Santos, also known as orishas in the Yoruba language, are "fed" his or her favorite food or sacrifice. Most common offering is the blood of roosters and goats. Birds such as pigeons, canaries or hens are used in rubbing rituals in which a believer is cleansed, with the notion that any evil present is passed into the birds.

Although Santeria permeates Spanish-speaking Miami, it usually remains hidden behind Main Street-style storefronts. The *Associated Press* reported that two grieving disciples met at a Miami funeral home to mourn their dead mentor, a sorcerer. "As one man lay with his head in his girlfriend's lap," the report continued, "police say the second pumped three bullets into his skull with a .38-caliber revolver." Police arrested the man on a first-degree murder charge and said Santeria was to blame for the slaying.

Miami Homicide Sgt. Luis Albuerne said that "it was a black magic thing. Apparently the murderer thought the victim had passed along to his spiritual godfather all the bad spells on his head, and that's why he had died."

Sociologists say that Santeria and Palo have become one of the survival tools for Cuban refugees living in the United States.

"Santeria seems to give people a faith, a hope," says O.R. Dathorne, a professor of Afro-American studies at the University of Miami. "I would say 40 percent of all Cubans here partake of Santeria. And only 5 percent would have a negative attitude."

Wildlife activist Jack Kassewitz Jr, says that the "primitive worship of gods through sacrifices of birds and animals has reached epidemic proportions in Dade County. Daily we receive reports and bodies of sacrificed animals and birds."

Kassewitz works with the National Wildlife Rescue Team and that group has offered a reward of $2,000 for information leading to the conviction of ritual animal killers.

But one of the Santerian high priests, identified by the AP as Rigoberto Zamora, defended the sacrifices. "This is a religion that is very old," he says. "It dates back to the slaves' time and we can't let it die."

Zamora and a band of Santeria believers printed fliers to teach the English-speaking public why their faith requires the ritual slaughter of birds, lambs, goats and deer. Zamora says the leaflets were distributed in Miami supermarkets to show why Santeria has a rightful place in Miami's ethnic and spiritual life.

"We are respectful of the law, but we should be allowed to practice our religion in our churches and in our homes,"

Zamora concludes.

But by no means is the practice of Santeria restricted to the Miami area. It exists wherever Cubans wander. In Atlantic City, N.J., police made 19 animal cruelty arrests in a blood-spattered apartment. Officers found a robed woman kneeling, surrounded by other worshippers dressed in blood-smeared clothing, while in the kitchen two women were standing over a sink, butchering chickens.

Strewn around the apartment were hundreds of chicken, duck and lamb parts, three lamb carcasses without legs and several live chickens and pigeons, along with buckets of blood and animal intestines.

The *New York Times* reported a case in the Bronx area of New York City in which police officers and agents of an animal protection agency raided a garage and confiscated 62 animals apparently being held for sacrfice by Santeria cultists.

Police said that they believed there were as many as 1,000 groups in New York City who practice rites involving the sacrifice of animals. The Bronx raid netted young goats and lambs and 56 fowl, including ducks, guinea hens, pigeons, roosters and chicks. In an adjoining house, officials found seven persons cleaning pieces of coconut, chopping herbs and wrapping large leaves into bundles in preparation for a religious rite.

Back in Miami, Ramirez has estimated that more than half the 507,000 Cubans in the county practice Santeria.

"It comes at times of stress — divorce or death or illness — or say, if someone wants some luck with a lady," Martinez says. "I say the number is so high because of all the people who try it." Many fewer are seriously devoted to it, he adds.

Most santeros are reluctant to talk to writers about their beliefs or what they do. But one who agreed to talk is Ernesto Pichardo, who told a *Times* reporter, "We don't care to hear what your opinion is. We give you a reading (by throwing cowrie shells) and tell you what's wrong, and you can believe it or not. The solution, usually, is killing a rooster or bathing with certain herbs, something like that. Then it's up to you to do it. I can't free you. I'm just the instrument."

Mercedes Sandoval, an anthropologist in Miami, says that Santeria has no moral code. "In Santeria the gods are neither good nor bad; they are brokers of power," she says. "You ask for things and you do things to get them. It's materialistic."

The religion has a number of saints, including Elegua, Chango and St. Barbara. Considered in human terms, the saints are linked with human experiences such as sex, wealth and wisdom. According to believers, the saints prefer different gifts. Such gifts, much like prescriptions, can be purchased at the botanicas. There are at least 30 such stores in Dade County, write Martinez and Wetli. They are rites and ceremonials. A rite can be performed by a person who is alone or in the company of a santero. A ceremonial, however, is a situation with more than two persons present and is always conducted by a santero.

Simple rites involve such things as lighting candles, offering glasses of water to the dead and to the orishas. Ceremonials, in contrast, can encompass a complex ritual performance.

Santerians believe in the utilization of modern medicine but often will seek to insure the success of the medical therapy by going to a santero for additional help. Practitioners of Santeria also believe in illnesses that do not respond to normal medical means. Santerians think that illnesses can result from the anger of the santos, from neglect of the dead, from the breaking of taboos and from a disrespectful or neglectful attitude toward the gods. As believers in malevolent or evil magic, practitioners turn to the santero, not the medical doctor, for cures to such ailments.

Santero treatment centers around the trabajo (work or job), which refers to magic performed to achieve a desired end

161

through the intervention of the deities and the dead. A brujeria or bilongo is a kind of trabajo connected with evil sorcery, achieved in ways such as giving a person a magical preparation in food and drink or when a spirit of the dead is "sent" with the intention of causing torment and misfortune to the victim. Other kinds of brujeria include depositing animal carcasses such as decapitated roosters, dead goats or human skulls at the doorway of a business or home. Sometimes special dolls are prepared and stuffed with ritual items such as pendants, herbs, or names of people. The dolls are kept at home, Martinez and Wetli outline a "typical" situation, in which a person complains to the santero that life circumstances are stressful. The santero will diagnose such problems as stemming from marital discord, an inability to work properly, muddled thinking or health problems primarily of a psychosomatic nature.

The santero, after diagnosing these conditions as a trabajo or brujeria will perform a despojo (the word is translated as "despoil") to remove the evil from the person. The despojo can include such techniques as suggestion, singing, screaming, observance of taboos and using rubbing rituals with herbs and flowers. Often the "ill" person can be returned to health through these measures.

One common remedy is a prayer of the head, called a rogacion de cabeza. Its aim is to exorcise spirits or evil. The rite lasts three days. The santero consults oracles to see if washing of the head is indicated. If the answer is affirmative, the santero will recommend what is needed, possibilities including the use of vegetables, herbs, oils, fruits, colognes and other items rubbed directly on the head. The materials are allowed to remain on the head for 72 hours. The believer performs this rite at home, by his or her self. Food taboos also are observed and there is an avoidance of sex and other activities through the period. At the end of three days, there is a ritual washing of the head. The rite can be repeated as often as it is necessary. Those who attempt this rite usually complain of psychological unrest, insomnia, confused and unclear thinking and fatigue.

In another rite, necklaces of the Seven African Powers (the important deities of Santeria) are worn in a rite that takes six weeks to prepare and can cost from $250 to $500. The necklaces are "fed" and "cleansed" by the santero, using tobacco smoke, blood, herbs, water and rum. The person being treated must wear white clothing for a month, covering the head with a white hat or shawl. There are food taboos and restrictions on sex and recreation.

To those who feel the "call" to become a santero, or priest, the road is long, complex and expensive. It can take a year to go through the process of gaining the title of santero. Expenses run from $2,000 to $5,000. Throughout the period there are many taboos, animal sacrifices and religious magic activities.

Godparents are chosen by the prospective santero, and they will train him throughout the year. The training process varies, although all initiates will wear white clothing for the entire training period, have a shaved head and observe food taboos. At the end of the training period, there is a final ceremony in which the new santero is reincorporated into the cultural life of his group. On that date every year thereafter, the santero will celebrate a "spiritual birthday."

The artifacts and items used in the practice of Santeria can be big business. One large botanica in Dade County stocks statues, pottery, beads and candles. Also on its shelves are scented oils and feathers. The store has refrigerated herbs. Gambler's Spray comes in an aerosol can, as does a Love Spray. Pigeons are kept in cages behind the store.

The Rev. Juan Sosa is a Catholic priest in Miami who is considered the leading authority on Santeria in the archdiocese. He is chairman of the Committee of Popular Piety.

One of its goals is bringing followers of Santeria into the church.

"I ask them to leave their Santeria symbols with me," Sosa says. "They need to be free of this bargaining — you get this, if you do that."

Another santero, Jorge Luis Acosa, was reluctant to talk to a reporter about his faith. He was offended that the Humane Society of Greater Miami had offered a $2,000 reward for information leading to the arrest of persons involved in animal rites. He found this close-minded and disrespectful. The religion is something important to him, something reverent.

"In the first day, there was the river ceremony," he says. "I was submerged, and my old clothes were disposed of, and I was dressed in white. When I was taken home to my god-father's, a chicken was decapitated and the blood was dropped on my head and my elbows and my knees. Then the same thing was done with cocoa butter and honey, and feathers were stuck to my body."

He said that he slept on the floor with two lit candles at his head. The following day he was covered with a white sheet and cleansed with a liquid of mashed herbs. Priests chanted songs of various saints. Acosa says that his head was shaved. His scalp was painted red, white, blue and yellow. Then came a ritual killing of animals, including a goat, guinea hen and pigeons.

He continued that for seven days. "I could not leave the room, except when I asked to be taken to the bathroom. Symbolically, I was like a child, being born again."

He describes the following year as one of chants and sacrifice. It was a quiet, secluded life. He says he was not permitted in the rain or the noonday sun. During this period he studied Santeria prayers written in the language of the Yoruba tribe.

He described himself as being "in jail for the saints." He adds that it is his "new life."

The black magic sect of Santeria, the Palo Mayombe, offers the greatest threat for law enforcement authorities, according to authors Wetli and Martinez. "For personal gain or a fee, they will perform rituals to inflict mental or physical harm, or even death, on an individual," the writers observe. "The practitioners are often locally reputed to be career criminals engaged in drug smuggling."

A basic tool used by these practitioners — often called paleros or mayomberos — is an iron cauldron filled with sacred dirt and containing human bones, blood, coins and other items.

Wetli and Martinez have said that "besides ritualistic death wishes, outright homicide and apparent natural deaths have been associated with Santeria rituals."

In one reported case, a farmer in the Miami area had an altercation with a Cuban tenant over property upkeep and the lack of care shown to the tenant's goats, pigs and chickens. The following morning, the farmer found a decapitated chicken on his front porch, along with a split coconut and 14 pennies. All of this was wrapped in white cloth. When the farmer went to the tenant's hut, he found an altar, in the center of which was an iron cauldron filled with dirt. Placed on top of the dirt was a goat skull, topped by a blood-drenched human skull. The human skull supported a chicken head. There was a chain draped across the front of the skull. At the left was a small doll with a tiny sword piercing its chest. There were deer antlers draped with a red ribbon, an antique sword and a machete behind the skull. Thrust into the dirt of the cauldron were two knives. The farmer saw that candles were burning in and around the cauldron. Candles placed on the floor depicted Saint Barbara. The scene also included a plywood board with a glyph drawn in chalk, a decapitated chicken and a section of railroad track. Hanging from the ceiling were strands of beads, most strands having just two colors. In front of the cauldron was a pan of water which contained two split coconuts, a turtle shell, and an intact coconut. A smaller cauldron contained dirt, railroad spikes, a knife, deer antlers, and a strand of yellow beads. Wound around the outside of the smaller cauldron was a chain with amulets of agricultural tools. A nearby box was filled with dirt, with a small plastic skeleton resting on top. There was an additional glyph chalked on a nearby wall. In a paper bag behind the door was a small figurine of the trickster god called Elegua.

The responsible santero denied that any of this outlay represented a malevolent aspect of Santeria. But experts Wetli and Martinez commented that it was typical of the black magic cult of Palo Mayombe. The tenant, who was dressed in white that is typical of a santero, had a receipt for the skull, which had been purchased at a botanica for $110. The receipt indicated that the skull was that of a 39-year-old African male and that it had been sold for educational purposes.

Florida has no law prohibiting possession of a skull, but it does forbid trafficking in human remains. However, no charges were filed against owners of the botanica. The santero was arrested and charged with animal cruelty because of the apparent neglect of living animals at the scene. No charges were filed for the ritualistic decapitation of the chickens or goats. The report concludes that the farmer, apparent target of the ritual, did not become sick or die in the ensuing months after the incident.

Another case involved grave diggers who went to a cemetery to complete work on a grave site that had been previously dug. They found two plastic bags, one containing a nearly complete skelton, the other a skull and some vertebrae. Chicken feathers and blood covered one of the skulls. Ends of some of the long bones had been sawed off. Officials never determined the source of the bones but were convinced that they had been used in the practice of Santeria. One theory was that the bones had been taken to the cemetery following the dismantling of a nganga, which is the source of power for the santero. Such action is often taken after a santero's death, to assure that no powers remain. Another guess was that the bones might have been part of a rejuvenation ritual for a nganga or that they were an offering to Oya, the African goddess who owns the cemetery.

There are numerous cases of graverobbings that may be blamed on practitioners of Santeria. Rituals are performed that require a skull with a decomposing brain be taken from a grave.

Wetli and Martinez write of the potential for violence and homicide in the practice of Santeria, relating a case in which a Cuban man was chased and shot several times by another Cuban. The victim died. His clothes were covered with a multicolored glitter, which also was found in his shoes. It was learned that he had practiced Santeria, often wore shoes that did not match and sometimes wore glasses with one dark lens and one clear lens. Police investigation revealed that three days prior to the shooting, the victim had threatened to cut off the head of his assailant and offer it to the saints. This demonstrates that the threats and beliefs of the Santeria cult are taken seriously by their adherents. There is a chance for violence against those who would reveal the secrets of Santeria or threaten santeros.

In another incident, a 42-year-old Cuban who was a defendant in a drug conspiracy trial visited his madrina (a Santera godmother) seeking a ceremony to cleanse his spirit. The woman allegedly threw dice which indicated that the trial would not go in his favor. The defendant was found dead the next morning. Although an autopsy showed that his death was due to natural causes — a heart malfunction secondary to high blood pressure — adherents to Santeria undoubtably would attribute the man's death to supernatural causes. To a Santerian, it would appear that the cleansing ceremony failed to appease the orisha (deity), thus bringing about punishment.

167

To believers, such a failure would result in bad luck or possibly in death.

It has been difficult to trace Santeria, since the religion does not have a bible. Many of its practitioners worship in secrecy, since they fear public ridicule or interference from the police.

Although Santeria most commonly is employed for good or neutral purposes, researchers do not dismiss the suggestion that it can be utilized by criminals as well. Palo Mayombe shares many similar beliefs and artifacts with Santeria, but most often is aimed toward malevolent sorcery. Palo Mayombe followers are devoted to brujeria, which is the use of human remains. This feature in particular distinguishes Palo Mayombe from other religions with African or Caribbean origins.

Palo Mayombe also is called Palo Monte. It originated in the Congo region of Africa. Much like the Yoruba culture from West Africa, which gave birth to Santeria, followers of Palo Mayombe were brought to Latin America as slaves. And like the followers of Santeria, the Congo slaves tried to blend their religion with the beliefs of their Spanish masters, who were Roman Catholics. There has been a mixing of Catholic saints with those brought over from Africa.

In Palo Mayombe, the principal deity is known by at least three titles: Guindoki, Chamalongo and Nsambi. This deity is the equivalent of the dieties Olofi or Olodurmare in Santeria.

Many santeros have claimed to have been initiated into the Palo Mayombe cult as well, and there are instances when religious paraphernalia of the two religions have been found in different parts of the same house.

But Palo Mayombe has features which distinguish it from Santeria, according to authors Wetli and Martinez. The principal difference is that the myths and rituals of the Palo Mayombe are concentrated in the spirit of the dead, known as the kiyumba. The magic performed is used to bring misfortune or death against an enemy.

If a palero performs benevolent or neutral magic, he or she may be called a mayomberos christianos. Those who try to work in malevolent sorcery are labeled mayomberos judios. Initiation requires purifying rituals, one of which includes wearing clothing buried in a grave three weeks earlier. The initiation winds up with the presentation of a scepter, called a kissingue, which consists of a human tibia wrapped in a black cloth. Such a scepter, paleros believe, rules over the powers of darkness.

According to Wetli and Martinez, "The ritual life of a palo Mayombe centers about the nganga, often referred to as the prenda ("jewel"). This sacred cauldron contains human bones (invariably a human skull, with or without long bones as well), sticks from the forest or wood ("palos de monte"), various herbs, feathers, railroad spikes, animal bones (skulls or other bones of various birds and sometimes turtles), small iron agricultural tools (rakes, picks, hoes, etc,), sacred stones, and other items which may be of special significance to the palero. The most important of these items are the sacred stones and the human skull. The stones are ritually 'fed' when the nganga is offered blood in a ceremony called simbankisi. The skull is specifically referred to as the kiyumba, meaning spiritual substance or intelligence of the dead. The 'father' or 'mother' of the nganga interacts with his/her kiyumba by 'feeding,' 'punishing' or making the nganga 'give birth' to initiates or new paleros. The skulls may be obtained from various sources. However, some mayomberos insist on a skull in which the brain is still present so the kiyumba can think and act better."

Other items which have ritual significance are contained in the nganga. According to Wetli and Martinez, "Gunpower 'fula' is used for divination purposes by placing small amounts in a row and observing how they burn. Sulfur is commonly used as an incense during the practice of malevolent sorcery. Azoque (quicksilver or mercury) is another important component since its ease of flow and movement is believed to vitalize and energize the nganga. Mercury is also used in conjunction with vulture feathers and the kiyumba to produce madness in an enemy. Ashes (mpolo banso) form another integral part of the nganga and are used for purification (when rubbed on the hands) and for defensive or aggressive magic."

Wetli and Martinez interviewed one devotee of Palo Mayombe, a 48-year-old Cuban who had been found to be the owner of an altar uncovered on a rural farm in Florida. At age 17, he suffered from epilepsy which did not respond to the use of santeros. His father took him to a palero, who cured him by making multiple incisions on his body and covering these with 21 pieces of wood. The epileptic seizures never returned, he said.

Since then, the man said he had been a devotee of Palo Mayombe but said he was not a palero. "The man indicated that the Palo Mayombe cult was separate and distinct from Santeria although, in his opinion, there has been a blending of the two religions in recent years. He further indicated that there were two separate cults of Palo Mayombe, one dealing entirely with evil magic (the majority) and the other dealing with white magic." The authors were told that the white magic altar always had a crucifix associated with it. He said the number 21 was significant to the cult but claimed he did not know why.

"He explained that the surgical instruments were there to symbolize success in recovery from surgery of a particular individual, and the cowrie shells were used for divination purposes," they report.

"He claimed to have purchased the skull and femur from a dentist in another state. Anthropologically the skull was consistent with that of East Indian origin which would be typical of a medical specimen. He explained that the femur symbolized walking and travel, symbolic of Taga Legua (the equivalent of Elegua, owner of the roads in Santeria.) The tibia is supposed to possess the real significance in this regard, but lacking a tibia, he used the femur."

Police officers have been advised to use extreme caution when dealing with practitioners of either Santeria or Palo Mayombe. An April 1987 article in *Police Magazine* suggested that officers carefully handle any religious artifacts, including altars, pictures, shrines, beads, incense, oils or statues in the home of believers. The magazine stated that mishandling, even when unintentional, could lead to a violent attack. It also must be again noted that adherents to either religion enjoy the freedom of religion guarantees of the First Amendment.

13

Paganism

Much has been written about witchcraft over the years. A lot of what has been published deals with the black aspects of the practice, with the use of sorcery and the black arts, to bring about evil purposes.

In my investigations of the entire area of the occult over the past years, I have interviewed many of those who profess to practice the ancient art of witchcraft. But mostly they claim to be "white" witches, those whose beliefs and rituals are aimed only toward beneficial results. Their aims, they assert, are only good ones.

Many of today's followers do not like being called "witches." They realize that the word witch brings with it all sort of negative ideas and forces. Today's white witches prefer to be called practitioners of Wicca, sometimes called Wicce, The Craft, or The Old Religion.

In June 1987, on the weekend of the summer soltice, I received permission to attend a goddess gathering — also called a festival — of practicing members of Wicca at a remote area in southeastern Ohio. Attending this event were approximately 125 Wiccans from across the eastern part of the United States, from New York to Florida. It was a bright, sunny and warm weekend. As I walked through the area, talking with various members of the covens who had assembled for this annual spring festival, the air was filled with the sounds of chirping birds. Those sweet noises blended with the laughter of young children romping and enjoying themselves while their parents assembled to indulge in a religion that they claim had its beginnings in Paleolithic times. The only thing that might cause an unprepared visitor to see this gathering as anything other than a large picnic was the fact that some of those wandering around the grounds were "skyclad," their description for going in the nude.

Two of the most interesting and articulate white witches who agreed to answer my questions were the husband-and-wife singing team who identify themselves as Kenny and Tzipora. They make their living as entertainers, "mainstream folk musicians who sell to the general public." But Kenny adds that they also are Wiccan, or pagan.

Tzipora defines a Wiccan as "wise one, or one who shapes things. The Wiccan religion is based on the natural cycles of the earth and all things related celestially. We work with the seasons, with the phases of the moon and with multiple facets of the creating energy, which we term god and goddess."

Kenny interrupts his wife to give his definition of paganism in general. "We worship the creator, just like Christian and Jews, but we see the creator of all things as being both male and female, since life was created both male and female. We term the female aspect of creation as the goddess, while the male aspect is the god. We do not see the goddess and the god as being above, in the heavens, but as being all around us in the earth."

Kenny says the difference between the dark and white crafts

is that of "night and day." He adds, "During the Middle Ages, the Catholic Church wanted to erase any religion that was not Catholicism. One was the pagan belief in the goddess and the god, especially the belief in the goddess, because it threatened the patriarchy, the male orientation of Christianity as the church practiced it. They conducted the witch hunt, in which they killed nine million people by torture. They took the words and the symbols which we use to define our religion. The Catholics were allowed to wage a massive propaganda campaign using those terms in a negative aspect.

"Our god has horns because he represents both people and horned animals. There are many names for our god, who is called in general terms the Horned God. Many cultures with many languages knew him, so there are many names. Among them are Pan, Kerninos, Mars, Zeus, Apollo, Thor, Odin. We do not worship many gods, but rather one god and one goddess who have many names.

"Just as Christ is called Jesus, or Emmanuel, or Christ, or the Lamb or the Lion, we have many names for our god and goddess. The Christian Church was able to wage this massive propaganda campaign for the past 2,000 years, taking our symbols and terminology use to create a new religion which was the opposite of Christianity. The Catholic Church, as practiced in the Middle Ages, believed that Christ was the good side of the world. They took the image of our Horned God and created a new term: Satan or the Devil. They took our symbols and connected them with Satan."

Kenny says that Satanists are not practicing the religion that Wiccans practice. He says his religion "is much older than Christianity, " Satanists are involved in a religion that is anti-Christian, the reverse of Christian. "In that way," he says, "Satanists are Christians. They are practicing the other side of Christianity (which is) the belief in a force of evil. We do not believe that any force in the universe, any force whatsoever, is inherently evil. We believe that people can use some forces to do evil, but all forces that are natural, that are created by the god and goddess, are neither good nor evil. They are just there. We can work good with them, or we can work evil with them, but they are just there."

I asked if they had had any experience with someone who practiced both the white and dark sides of witchcraft.

Tzipora replied, "Do you think it's possible that someone who lives a good Christian life, who follows the word of Christ, could possibly be a wife beater and a child molester?" Then, she answers her own question, "It is absolutely possible."

She continues that such a person is not accepted by other Wiccans "any more than a wife beater or child molester is accepted by other Christians."

Kenny explains that there is not much that Wiccans can do to prevent such occurrences, "since we do not have a central organization or a seminary." He says that when they know of someone who is practicing the black arts, such a person is banned from their gatherings and their covens. "We will publicly state that we do not associate with them."

But, Tzipora adds, "That's about as far as we can go." There are no enforcement agencies within the craft, Kenny explains. But such persons are "usually ostracized" by the community of white witches.

"If it is somebody who is not desirable, then we find ways to exclude them from our public activities," Tzipora says.

Kenny goes on to detail an experience the couple went through several years ago. "A fellow for a long time claimed to be worshipping what he called the black aspect of the god Pan," Kenny says. "Everyone was a little leery of this, but he seemed to be a pagan and he was generally accepted. But then he began doing some really questionable things. He was accused of rape, he was accused of stealing. Finally he admitted that he was a Satanist. Since then he has been banned from any pagan activity."

Kenny says that Wiccans are pantheistic. "We believe that all things of the earth are part of the creator." Tzipora admits that it would be wonderful if there were Wiccans located across the country who could "go public" and tell their story to the media. Kenny says that there are such persons, but that the media seems interested only on special occasions, such as Halloween. "All the newspapers want an interview with a witch then," he says. "But we exist 365 days a year." There's a lack of followup, he adds, stating that the couple had been interviewed by a reporter two years ago. He says the published story was accurate and well done but that there was no followup. "They never came back to us whenever other stories were published about witches killing people. They never came back to ask what our point of view as witches might have been."

The couple discussed the importance of celebrating the summer solstice. "This is on the solar calendar what a full moon is like on the lunar calendar," Tzipora says. "The sun is at its zenith. This is the time when we can see the work we have put into crops. To those of us who live in the cities, we can see the results of what we have been working on, since we labor in an actual growth cycle. Summer solstice is a time of caring for our 'crops,' as opposed to working hard at getting the crops. In a sense, summer solstice is a lull, since we can sit back and celebrate all the things we have been working on."

Kenny notes that the sabbats coincide with the extreme positions of the sun: solstices, equinoxes and cross quarters. For instance the spring equinox is called Ostara, which he says was appropriated by the Catholic church and called Easter, which Kenny says is essentially the same word. Ostara's original meaning was "welcoming back life to the earth."

Tzipora says Ostara is the time when the "young lord and the young lady — the god and goddess in their young aspects — are together."

Kenny says that Wiccans "revere all life. Most pagans feel guilty about squashing a bug. A good pagan who follows the two sets of laws we have — the Wiccan Read and the Charge of the Goddess — would never consider taking a life."

The Wiccan Read, Kenny says, is a set of laws which comes from ancient times. It is very simple and culminates in saying "Ye harm none, do what ye will," meaning that one can do anything as long as it harms no other living thing,

The Charge of the Goddess is allegedly the word of the goddess, saying basically that believers must worship the goddess, respect all life on earth because she put it there, and that believers must gather on the sabbats and the full moons to meet together and worship her.

Originally, Halloween was called Samhain, a Celtic celebration that honored the ghosts of warriors who had died. It was practiced on October 31, because of the position of the sun indicated to Wiccans that this was a time when the physical world was closest to the other world, where those who had died then existed. It is a concept close to the Christian concept of heaven, although Kenny says they don't believe in rewards after death. "We believe that when people die, they just go to the next place."

When Catholics "took over" the concept of Samhain, or Halloween, they "pretty much kept the idea the same, that of honoring those dead who are sacred or hallowed. The reason children dress up as ghosts is to honor those who have died."

Catholics worship those who are holy or sainted at Halloween. Thus Satanists chose the same time to honor the powers of evil. Satanists believe they can "open the veil" and bring in the forces of evil from another world at that time.

The moon symbolizes the goddess, Tzipora observes. "The sun is masculine and the moon is feminine," she says. The Charge of the Goddess instructs believers that once a month, "and better it be when the moon is full," they gather in a

"secret glade and worship me, the queen of all mysteries."
The full moon is when the goddess is strongest and her power
is at the fullest. "It is then we get together to worship and
celebrate that energy," Tzipora says. "She also says that if
we ask anything of her on the full of the moon, that our wish
will be granted. Our worship and all this is nothing more than
our way of praying and acknowledging the power that created
us."

Satanism is "ripping off" the pagans' beliefs about the
power of the moon. Tzipora says Satanists are foolish in having their ceremonies when the moon is full, since it would
make more sense to do something evil in the dark, rather than
during the bright light of a full moon. Satanism should plan
its rites during the dark side of the moon, when the tides are
not moving in full force, when it is more difficult to discern
what is occurring.

The true story of Wiccan or paganism today doesn't get
told, Kenny and Tzipora contend, simply because of fear.
"Many members of our community do not want to come out
and say that Satanism is not about us," Kenny says, "because
of prejudice. Many of our believers live in communities where
their jobs, social standing and relations with neighbors would
be destroyed were they to admit their Wiccan beliefs."

Kenny says that because he and his wife are entertainers
and travel around the country, they are in a better position
to talk about their beliefs. "We don't have to worry as much
as someone who is a teacher or works in a public office. We
can come out and talk a little freer than most people."

Kenny believes that witches face harm because of Christian teachings. "The Bible has a line that says 'thou shalt not
suffer a witch to live.' That line was not in the original Bible
as given to the Jews 5,000 years ago. It was put into the Bible
during the witchcraft persecutions by a pope who wanted the
competition destroyed."

Tzipora says that this is a time-honored political kind of

move. "If you want to take over, the first thing you do is turn the other side into something evil. Once you have established fear, it is easy to build on that fear. Fear is a great force. Witches don't want to come out of the broom closet because they are afraid."

"People don't know who we are," Kenny says, "so they are afraid of us." The Wiccan says a former Jehovah's Witness had visited their home recently and confessed that if he were still a member of the Witnesses, he would not have listened to the story of paganism and would have run out of the house because of what he had been taught that witches are.

"People like stereotypes. They like to think that all witches kill on the full of the moon. They like to think that witches have a long nose with a wart on it."

The couple denies reports of sexual orgies at witches' gathering. "The naturalists have the same problem," Tzipora says. "Just because you take your clothes off does not mean that you automatically have sex."

Kenny says that Wiccans are "a little bit freer" than the general public. Many believe in nudism. "When we are outside in a natural environment with woods and trees, we see nothing wrong in taking our clothes off and living the way people, we feel, were intended to live; without clothing. Because we take our clothes off does not mean that we are going to jump upon the first member of the opposite sex we see and wham it in there. We are very respectful of people's sexual and physical needs. We do not impose ourselves sexually on anyone who is not willing."

The Charge of the Goddess says that to be truly free, "you shall be naked in your rites." Tzipora says it is difficult to feel inhibited and to do something negative when one is naked. "It's all out there. Psychologically, removing your clothes means you have removed your uniform, your mask."

Kenny points out that clothing also still denotes social rank.

179

By removing one's clothes, there is no way of knowing one's social rank, "You are truly free; you don't have social stigmas when you are naked."

Both Kenny and Tzipora wear pentacles around their necks. I asked them about the pentacle's significance.

"The five-pointed star represents earth, air, fire, water and spirit over all," Tzipora replies. "It also is the symbol of man within the universe."

Kenny says, "Imagine it as a person with his legs outstretched and his arms cast up to the heavens and his face looking upward."

Both also wear tattoos on the inside of their arms. "This is a personal choice that we made," Kenny says, "as a commitment to our religion and our coven. Each member of the coven, upon reaching a certain level of competence within the craft, is tattooed." The tattoo includes a seven-pointed star, which Tzipora says is "tied in with the seven mystical planets." There also is a circle "that contains the knowledge" and a crescent moon that represents one who has attained the third or teaching degree within paganism.

"We do not proselytize," Kenny emphasizes. "We never go and tell people that they should or must become a pagan."

Tzipora claims that pagans "are very much like the Masons" in their refusal to seek new members. "A Mason may not come up to you and say, 'Hi, do you want to join?' You have to ask."

Kenny says pagans believe that all religions are valid. "We respect Christianity, Buddhism, Islamism. We believe that people have to make their own choices about which religious path they want to follow. Because of that, we cannot proselytize. But if someone comes to us and says, 'Teach me,' then we teach them as much as we know."

I asked how long it takes to become a witch. Kenny replied that the training period varies from group to group. "Within our coven the minimum amount of time for a typical student

180

is about a year. We have eight sabbats that represent the equinoxes, the solstices, and the four cross quarters of the positions of the sun. They are approximately six weeks apart. There also are 13 full moons each year. After a person has seen all the eight sabbats and all the full moons, in our tradition, they qualify to ask to be initiated, to become a witch. Before that a person who worships the god and goddess and has not been initiated is not a witch but a pagan. One is initiated when he receives what we call the power, basically when one attains a certain level of competence in working with the worship of the goddess and god. One must know how to direct energies into the great energy of the creation. Then one becomes a witch, which signifies clergy. It is the same as being called a priest, a priestess, a rabbi or a teacher.''

In the system subscribed to by Kenny and Tzipora, there are three degrees. ''When you become a witch, you are a first degree, and you are entitled to all the workings of the group you have come into,'' Kenny says. ''After approximately a year, you are entitled to second degree, at which you start to learn techniques with which to teach other people. The culmination is third degree, when you are allowed to go out and teach other people how to become witches.''

I ask them what they do when someone offends them. ''Do witches reach into a black bag when someone does something against them?'' I question.

''One of the laws we live by,'' Kenny responds, ''is the Law of Three. Christians believe that Christ will forgive anything one does. But we believe that anything you do will come back to you three times. If I were to cast a spell on you, something evil, I believe that that negative energy would come back to me three times. Why would I do something bad to you, if three bad things will happen to me because of it? In my right mind, I would never dream of it, unless I was very masochistic. Because of our law, a sane person

181

would not knowingly do anything evil. Your average witch will never do a spell that is inherently evil. The Charge of the Goddess says, 'Ye harm none do what ye will.' We are not allowed to harm any life form.''

I asked them about Anton LaVey, leader of the Church of Satan.

Tzipora answers. "First of all, Anton LaVey is a very, very good businessman," she says. "Uncle Anton just knew a good thing when he saw it. He recognized that people in today's society like themselves. He thought if he could sell them on the idea of worshipping themselves, he could make a lot of money. And he did.

"I happen to know many members of the Church of Satan. Things may have changed since I was last in touch — six or seven years ago — but at the time I knew these folks, I was led to believe that LaVey does not practice Satanism as it is established in the media. He does not propose that people go out and kill animals. There are only two holidays in their calendar. The first is Walpurgis Night, which coincides with Beltane, or May Eve. The second is one's birthday. The Church of Satan is a hedonistic system based on attainment of things for one's self.''

Kenny interrupts, "They would be the kind of people to organize orgies, because it feels good.''

Tzipora says that she sees the hedonistic attitude espoused by the Church of Satan exemplified in corporations. "People do it in big business all the time, and no one calls them Satanists. That is really what Anton meant. He did not mean that one should go out and kill those he doesn't like. Unfortunately, people misinterpret him.''

Kenny again speaks. "Let me point out that in Christianity, which sees Christ as a God who is only love and goodness, there is in the Bible a line which says, 'Thou shalt not suffer a witch to live.' This specifically means, if someone is not Christian, you have the right to kill them. Just like Anton

182

LaVey, the Bible says if someone is not of your faith, go kill them. Do people take this seriously? I hope not.''

Tzipora says, "This is not a religious issue, this is a law enforcement issue. Breaking the law is breaking the law. It has nothing to do with a religious issue.''

Both Kenny and Tzipora deny that Anton is a witch, although LaVey wrote a book titled The Compleat Witch.

"There is a movement in paganism,'' Kenny says, "to stop using the word witch because there are so many negative connotations. When we speak publicly, Tzipora and I, we say that we are pagans, that we are Wiccans. If asked, 'Are you witches?' we say 'yes' because we were pagans who were initiated as clergy and therefore have the right to call ourselves witches. But we don't always call ourselves that. We are pagans.

"Our definition of witch is the original definition. LaVey's definition was generated by the Catholic Church, which wanted evil associated with that term.'' Asked about The Satanic Bible, Kenny points out that the word bible is a Christian term. "We do not have a bible,'' he says, "We have the Wiccan Read and the Charge of the Goddess. We do not follow the Bible. LaVey, by using the word bible, implies to me that he is setting up a religion that is compatible to or opposite Christianity.''

I pointed out that in almost every murder case or crime involving Satanism, a copy of The Satanic Bible has been uncovered.

Tzipora responds, "I would guess that you probably have as many cases in which a person will tell you they committed a crime because an angel spoke to them. Or God spoke to them.''

Kenny mentions a group calling itself the Army of God. Members bomb abortion clinics in the name of God. "I would say the issue exists on both sides,'' Tzipora remarks.

She adds that the issue of *The Satanic Bible* is not an easy one. "I am against censorship, so I don't want to see any effort made to censor that book. But I do think that it would be nice that our kids be educated about possible pitfalls, making very clear to them what all these sects really are about."

"Wicca doesn't tell you that your spiritual responsibility is shouldered by a rabbi or priest or a god," Tzipora says. "You as an individual are completely and singularly responsible for your own spiritual growth."

"Christ said that those who have ears, let them hear; those who have eyes, let them see. I feel the same way," Kenny says. "There are people in society who have been indoctrinated into a code that does not allow them to believe that any religion but their own is okay."

Kenny insists that he does not want to entice people into his religion. "I don't want to make people pagans if they don't want to be pagans. But I want to let people know that we are okay, that we don't kill people, that we don't eat babies, we don't sacrifice animals, we don't make parchment out of skin. We are a religion. We worship our gods. We ask nothing from anyone other than that they respect that."

Both Kenny and Tzipora wear small cloth bags around their neck. They explain that the bags were gifts from a gathering in Wisconsin. The bags contain herbs and a crystal. "We all wore them to show that we were part of a village. We had a small community of several hundred there. The bags were sort of identification badges."

Kenny says that many pagans, because they worship the creation and the natural forces of the earth, are interested in using plants to heal illnesses, help people medicinally, to make teas, etc. This is one "path of power," in which pagans take the natural creation that the god and goddess gave them, using it to help themselves. Some pagans also believe in crystals, which are formed in the earth, for healing, to channel energies. The crystal itself does not heal, but serves as a focus for natural healing.

Some pagans believe that fire can be used as a focus to pray, to ask the god and goddess for a particular favor, "In the Old Testament, God told the Jews to burn animals if they wanted something," Kenny says. "We don't burn animals, we just burn a candle."

I mention that perhaps pagans could be helpful to law enforcement agencies in fighting the tremendous problems caused by Satanism. Many times, I note, witches are blamed for something that was not their fault. In talking to them, I say, the idea is to put the light of truth on them, not to convince people to become pagans.

"We don't want converts," Kenny says. "We do not want people to leave the spiritual path that is right for them to come to ours. We only want people who truly believe that this is the correct thing for them to be doing. We respect all other religions. If you want to be a Chrisitian, I respect that. And I believe you should live by the word of Christ if that is your decision. I live by the word of the goddess. I do not believe in Heaven or Hell. I believe that my spirit, my soul, will become part of the goddess, part of the natural energy of creation and be channeled into whatever is next. I'm not wise enough to know what is next."

Tzipora points out that pagans believe in reincarnation. "It must occur. We must come back and do more," she says.

"We believe that your soul lives forever; it cannot be destroyed," Kenny says. "We believe that because of that, there are certain lessons that the soul must learn. It must come back in different lives as men and as women, as animals, plants, trees, whatever. I am not wise enough to know what will happen to my soul after I have died. The goddess knows. I trust her."

They believe that man creates his own heaven and hell. "You create a life for yourself in which you are unhappy, miserable and suffering," Kenny says, "or you can create a life for yourself where you are happy. But I do not believe there is a place where my soul can go that is evil."

Both Kenny and Tzipora were born Jewish. "Culturally I will never be anything but Jewish," Tzipora says. "That is a psychological and sociological impossibility. I was raised in a Jewish household, and I have Jewish values."

"But I don't see a problem," Kenny says. "Before 5,000 years ago, before the Jews believed that the Ten Commandments were given to Moses, the Jews were pagan and they had a goddess. You can be a good Jew, follow all the tenets of the Old Testament and worship your god if you consider your god to be a goddess. My family was never religious. I am the only religious member of my family. My mother accepts it."

Tzipora says, "My mother was much more accepting than my father has been. One of my brothers is a flat-out agnostic, and the other is a Jew by choice, by birth and by habit.

"They live in New York City, which is not as liberal-minded as many people think it is. Sometimes it's difficult. We have a daughter who attends public school." They are members of the Blue Star coven, which has nine active members.

Tzipora says she has "hived off" six covens, by reaching the third degree and qualifying as a teacher to begin new covens. Blue Star has existed as a traditional coven for 10 years. Tzipora has been involved in paganism for 15 years, while Kenny has been a believer for six years.

Many pagan groups have received recognition as churches. Such groups are open to being contacted by law enforcement agencies and offer whatever help they can to law officers.

In 1486 two inquisitors published a book called, *Malleus Maleficarum* (Hammer of Witches). According to Kenny, this was a, "guidebook to torturing witches." The book was regarded upon publication as the leading authority on witchcraft. It contained a dozen questions to be asked of suspected witches.

The book said that there were four points required of witches: renunciation of the Catholic faith, devotion to all evil, the offering of unbaptised children to Satan and total indulgence of lust.

Kenny says that when the dozen questions were posed to a suspect, that person would be continually tortured until he or she came up with the "appropriate answers."

"So the question would be, 'Do you worship Satan?' If the person said, 'No,' they would be tortured until they said 'yes.'

"Thus the results were fixed."

Kenny and Tzipora call untrue books which claim that witches read tarot cards, foretell the future or fly through the air on brooms. "That's not true. But some witches enjoy reading tarot cards, some witches enjoy divination (ways of seeing the future), some witches enjoy hands-on healing, but those things are not necessary to being a witch. The only requirement of a witch is worshipping the goddess and the god."

Tzipora says the only thing important is the religion, and that any magic is a by-product. "By magic we don't mean lights coming out of our hands, but of creating change through conscious decision," they emphasize. "We mean the same thing that a Christian means in saying prayer: praying to the goddess and god for something to happen."

Tzipora relates an amusing anecdote. A decade ago she operated an occult shop in New York City. She was having a terrible problem with shoplifting. The usual sign that warned that shoplifters would be prosecuted to the full extent of the law did nothing to deter her losses. The item most favored by the thieves were small bottles of oil samples. The bottles were placed near the cash register and apparently were easy to palm and steal.

"Everybody knew I was a witch," she says. "After all, I operated an occult shop. To get rid of the shoplifting problem, as a joke I went to a pet store, bought a fish bowl, filled it with water and placed three newts in it. I put a little sign in front of the bowl which read, 'Former Shoplifters.' I never had another problem."

Kenny says, "That's magic. Magic is suggesting something to people's fears."

Tzipora says that she has used sympathetic magic, involving dolls or wax candles, to achieve a purpose. But she stresses again that such magic is employed only for good. "Dolls are very good for fertility," she says. "I've known many women who want to get pregnant. Make a doll that looks as much like them as possible and make it pregnant."

"But we never do any kind of magic unless a person asks that it be done," Kenny says. "And the magic we do is healing, helping women to get pregnant, helping to grow things, helping animals heal."

Another practitioner of paganism I interviewed during this Summer Solstice gathering calls herself Feather. She too has a longtime involvement with the religion. We have talked on several occasions over the years.

"The greeting among pagans is 'Blessed be,' " she tells me. Those not involved in the craft are labeled mundane. She says that many members give themselves an "occult name," which is a name other than their actual one. "Feather is my occult name," she says, "and many people in the occult community here don't know my real name."

Feather agrees with the statements by Kenny and Tzipora that pagans do not believe in the devil. "We think there are spirits out there who may cause great mischief. But we don't believe that Satan exists; therefore he cannot hurt us. We don't believe in any kind of negative magic, anything that will harm, injure or kill."

She also mentions what she calls the "Law of Threefold," in that anything a witch does good will come back to that witch three times. "Anything bad you do will also manifest itself three times, so you don't do anything bad because it will come back to you. That's the reason we never do it. A Satanist will draw upon the black path, call upon negative forces. But we don't. When we call down the deities inside the circle, we will call on archangels of the heavenly realm. We do not use or pay homage to dark deities. We do not recognize them."

She compares the "force" with the "Star Wars" film trilogy. If you have the force, it is a neutral power. "It's how you use that force that makes it good or bad."

Feather wears a cord or black belt. In some covens, pagans wear it tied around the head or around the chest. Many cords resemble drapery sashes. The color denotes degrees: white for high priestess, red for first degree, brown for second degree. Colors can differ depending on covens. Robes are worn for rituals and colors can differ by covens.

"Robes are worn for uniformity," she says. "It prevents distraction when we are working seriously in the circle. The colors have no relationship with Satanisn." Satanism and paganism are similar in that both use a ritual knife called the athame. Feather showed her knife to me. It contains her name, Feather, in the Theban language on the right hand side of the black handle. She says its positioning has no significance.

The other side contains Feather's magical number, which is seven. There is a crescent moon, a sun, a star and the sign of Cancer (her birth sign). Another sign, which to me looks similar to a symbol used by the brujeria black magicians of Africa and Latin America, signifies the soul and the spirit.

Feather points out that the athame "has not been used for any kind of killing. Ours is for calling down the deities, casting circles, or carving candles." She says it is a sacred tool.

"Some covens use a sword to cast their circle, but we do not. We use our athames to call down the deities and our wands to cast the circle."

Feather wears a sash, which she says demonstrates that she has passed two tests toward attaining the first degree. She has acted as a high priestess within a circle, has called down the deities and has cast the circle herself.

She says there are five different groups within the white craft today: Druidism, Traditionalists, Eclectic, Celtic (from the Welsh) and Gardnerian (following the teachings of Gerald Gardner, who believed that clothes interfered with the practice of religion).

Feather says she uses sea salt as a purifying element before she goes into a circle. "You wouldn't go to church with dirty hair, would you? That's not paying due respect to the Lord. That's the way we feel. We're not paying due respect if we're not clean."

She says all different colors of robes can be worn. "We wear anything we feel comfortable in. At a festival, anything goes."

I also spoke to Lady Brigid, a high priestess who lives in Central Ohio. She denies that today's Druids offer up human or animal sacrifices.

"We offer up sacrifices, but it's like giving a portion of your food," she says. "We will sacrifice part of something that we have."

However she admits that if a Druid did make an animal sacrifice, he or she would not be ostracized by the rest of the community. "That person would simply be practicing verbatim, and would be reverting to the old religion. It is not a Satanical thing; they do not offer sacrifices to Satan."

Prefacing her statements that an explanation is difficult to offer, she says, "There is a time and a place for that. But it is not something that is commonly practiced among any of the traditions." The traditionalist branch of witchcraft, she says, is almost as strict as the Gardnerians, whom she identifies as the most strict of the five classifications. "Their disciplines, rights, ways, are all done a specific way. There is no leniency. But the traditionalists believe that they are following the old ways."

She vociferously denies that any of the five branches practice any sort of sacrifices. "We cannot harm an animal. Some of us will not think twice about smashing a spider, but most of us try not to. We don't pick a flower, we don't cut down a tree, unless we have gotten into the energies of that flower or tree, asking, 'May I pick you?' or, 'May I cut you?' We get a feeling if it is all right or not. Our teachings are always to try to do something good for others and ourselves."

She says that pagans believe that self comes first. "You always have to be good to yourself. Your body is considered a temple. That has to be first and foremost."

During rituals she says that a circle is drawn to keep out "negative forces," although she says these are not the same as demons believed in by Satanists. "Negative forces can prevent your ritual from being successful," she says. "That negative energy can enter you if your aura is open. You might get a cold, flu or another kind of illness. It could affect your mental wellbeing. Negative forces could influence you adversely in many ways." Gardnerians are a quiet, reserved and non-public group, she says. They avoid publicity.

Celtics, however, are very ceremonial in their practices.

The eclectics, she says, are a melting pot of the other four categories. "Eclectics have to know what they're doing, because they are borrowing from the other four traditions. They must know what they are borrowing, what it is used for and how it's used because they can incorporate it in their rituals.

"We all have to know what we are doing, because in doing magic you must take responsibility. That's why there are teachers, to guide the students."

Lady Brigid, fearing retribution, keeps her real identity a secret in the city where she lives. "I have a husband and two children to think about. I don't want to put my husband's job in any jeopardy. I don't want my children to go through any persecution."

She says she has lived in the area for nine years. At first she was open about her membership in Wicca. "But I lost a lot of friends. It was the wrong thing to do, to admit it. In my home town of Chicago, I was very well known. Here, I couldn't do it. I realized I had to hide in the closet."

Lady Brigid claims she has gotten a raw deal from the news media. "I am used to being misquoted. I am used to being taken out of context. This is what happens. I have done a lot with television before. They can shoot 30 minutes of film, then they edit that 30 minutes down to three. Television sensationalizes everything."

I asked her about published reports that initiation into witchcraft requires blindfolding and flogging. She hesitates, then says, "I can't answer that. There is a vow of silence that we take on certain matters. I can't break those vows. But some of what you read is bogus. A lot of what is published in books is wrong. But some of it is fact. You have to be able to read between the lines."

When I question her about Satanist Anton LaVey, she laughs and describes him in somewhat raw terminology. "His books scared the heebie-jeebies out of me when I was still a novitiate," she adds. "Anton LaVey is a person who says one thing and does another. He is two-sided, two-faced and not to be trusted."

14

Signs and Symbols

HEBREW ALPHABET

א ALEPH (A) Ox 1	ב BETH (B) House 2	ג GIMEL (G) Camel 3	ד DALETH (D) Door 4	ה HE (H) Window 5	ו VAU (V) Peg, Nail 6	ז ZAYIN (Z) Weapon 7	ח CHETH (CH) Enclosure 8	ט TETH (T) Serpent 9
YOD (I) Hand **10**	**CAPH** (K) Palm of the Hand **20**	**LAMED** (L) Ox-Goad **30**	**MEM** (M) Water **40**	**NUN** (N) Fish **50**	**SAMEKH** (S) Support **60**	**AYIN** (O) Eye **70**	**PE** (P) Mouth **80**	**TZADDI** (TZ) Fishing Hook **90**
QOPH (Q) Back of Head **100**	**RESH** (R) Head **200**	**SHIN** (SH) Tooth **300**	**TAV** (TH) Sign of Cross **400**	**ך** Final Caph **500**	**ם** Final Mem **600**	**ן** Final Nun **700**	**ף** Final Pe **800**	**ץ** Final Tzaddi **900**

PAFSING THE RIVER

WRITING CALLED MALACHIM

CELESTIAL WRITING

194

RUNE ALPHABET

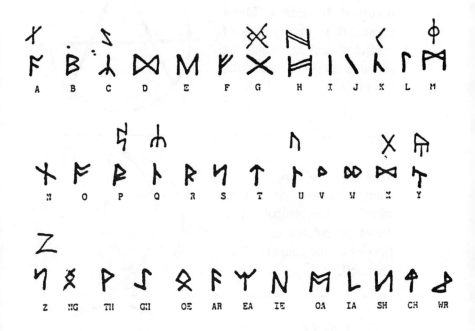

THEBIAN ALPHABET

This symbol is used by those involved in Heavy Metal Music. It is the symbol of "anarchy" and represents the abolition of all law and rules of society.

This symbol represents animals as well as human sacrifices. This symbol can be drawn or painted on rocks, trees or on the animal or victim itself.

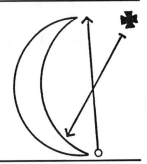

The inverted pentagram represents the baphomet which is the goat's head or it also represents Satan and the Anti-Christ's domination over the Father, Son and Holy Spirit.

In the '60s this was a peace symbol; in the '80s it is the "Cross of Nero". It represents an upside down cross with the broken cross members signifying the defeat of Christianity among the occultists.

196

The Swastika was used by the Nazis' SWP group. When turned in this direction, it represents the elements or forces turning against nature. The occult groups that use this symbol are opposed to Christianity. They are known as practitioners of Nazi Occultism.

The upside down cross means only one thing—blasphemy of Christianity and what it stands for, Jesus Christ.

The upside down cross with a question mark on it is better known as the Cross of Confusion, questioning Christianity. This is an ancient Roman symbol.

The triangle or power cone is placed on the ground and can be of different sizes and shapes. It is used to confine the demonic force that is conjured up during the Satanic rituals.

The double bladed ax is used in the death ritual. It is painted on the body of the deceased to send them off. It can also be used to represent anti-justice when inverted.

The magic circle has many different meanings. It can be used just as the triangle to confine the demonic or negative forces that are conjured up. They are normally smaller than the triangles. It is also used in rituals where the altar is set up inside a large circle. The magic circle symbolizes eternity, as well as protection against demonic or negative forces.

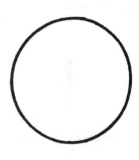

666 refers to the mark of the beast that is found in the Book of Revelation 13:16-18. The beast is the Anti-Christ or the Son of Satan.

The Satanic Salute is also known as the Devil's Triad. This salute is always given with the left hand.

The Black Mass Indicator indicates that a Black Mass was or is going to be performed.

The hexagram is not to be confused with the Star of David. This is also referred to as the Seal of Solomon. It is the most powerful symbol used by occultists.

When the symbol of the Goddess Diana, a crescent moon, is turned to face in this direction towards the symbol of Lucifer (which means "morning star"), a star, it is Satanic.

The Pentacle is used primarily by the White Craft, with the points having specific meanings. The points represent earth, fire, water, wind, spirit.

ASTROLOGICAL SYMBOLS

SOL - SUNDAY

LUNA — MONDAY

MARS — TUESDAY

MERCURY - WEDNESDAY

JUPITER -THURSDAY

VENUS - FRIDAY

SATURN - SATURDAY

SABBATS OR CELEBRATIONS

Satanists and witches celebrate eight holidays during the year. There are four major holidays called Sabbats and four minor holidays calles Esbats. In addition, Satanists hold a member's birthday in reverence.

February 2nd	-	Candlemas
March 21st	-	Spring Equinoxe
April 30th	-	May Eve or Beltane
June 22nd	-	Summer Solstice
August 1st	-	Lammas
September 21st	-	Fall Equinoxe
October 31st	-	Halloween - All Hallows Eve
December 22nd	-	Winter Solstice

The most significant of these major Sabbats are:

Halloween - All Hallows Eve

May Eve or Beltane

Summer Solstice

Winter Solstice

15

Conclusion

This book was not intended to be an exhaustive study of occultism and paganism. Rather it is one individual's personal experiences as an investigator, consultant and law enforcement officer.

The reader will notice that many of the interviews published have been conducted with persons whose philosophies and beliefs are in direct opposition to my own. But I felt that it was important that these persons' beliefs and their religions be published in an unadulterated manner. By giving these people the opportunity to state their cases, I think greater understanding by all will be the result. It is only with understanding that people will recognize situations that arise with the various groups discussed in this volume.

My point is that only through knowledge can we be equipped to deal with the problems presented by the occult. The objective of "The Satan Hunter" has been to open the eyes of readers, to impart wisdom and information for discerning the truth of the beliefs of the various groups discussed in these pages.

Each day I receive more information about occult occurrences both in the United States and throughout the world. As work on this book comes to an end, my files continue to expand with new reports coming in constantly. It seems that new groups, new cults, are being formed almost daily. Unless the general population is made aware of how to deal with such groups, then the chances are great that we will fall prey to their tactics.

I go back to an old saying that has stayed with me over the years. Before I was shipped to Vietnam to serve my country, I remember a sign that was prominently displayed in our guerrilla training camp. That sign read, "To kill a tiger, you must learn the ways of a tiger." Of course, I do not advocate killing anyone, but to fully understand the problem, you must understand the nature of the enemy.

Some of the destructive religions described in this book are the enemy. They are a threat to us. You must remember that as far as they are concerned, if you are not with them, you are against them. And if you are not one of them, then you are the enemy.

If this book can save one person's life, or help one person to be aware of the secretive and sometimes dangerous nature of cults, and the occult, then it has made the years of research worthwhile.

Appendix

A BRIEF DICTIONARY OF SATANIC TERMS

A.A. — Stands for Argenteum Astrum (Silver Star); Aleister Crowley founded this order in 1904.

ALTAR — The table used in rituals, it can be in the form of a table, tombstone, limestone, wood or a female, depending on the coven.

AMENON — Rules all spirits of the East.

ANKH — An Egyptian symbol.

ATHAME — A dagger or knife used in the ritual ceremony; a regular butcher knife can be used.

ANTICHRIST — Is seen as the son of Satan. In the book of Revelation, he will receive his powers from Satan.

BAPHOMET — At one time was worshiped by the Knights Templar and later by those who took part in the black mass. Today it is seen as a deity, a goat-headed god with angelic wings, the breasts of a female, and an illuminated torch between his horns.

BEELZEBUB — Recognized as the prince of demons.

BELIAL — This demon is the most vicious of all demons. He is identiified with death and evil. He is a demon of destruction.

BELTANE — A fertility festival held on May Day (May 1). It is one of the witches' major sabbaths.

BLACK MAGIC — Magic that is used for destruction, hate.

BLACK MASS — The most diabolical ritual that is performed by the Satanist. It is a communion with Satan, involving the desecration of all sacred objects used in the Christian communion. It also can include the sacrifice of an unbaptized infant.

BLOOD — Is the life force. The Satanist believes that by drinking another person's blood or the blood of an animal it will transfer that life force to the Satanist, magnifying the force by several times.

CAULDRON — A large pot used even today by practitioners. The opening in the cauldron represents the female womb. The cauldron is a very sacred object to practitioners.

CHALICE — A goblet, which can be made of glass or metal but is always silver in color. Among Satanists, gold is the symbol of righteousness.

CIRCLE — Very important among those involved in the black arts. The circle is their protection from the forces they conjure up in their incantations. It also is a symbol of totality and is used in ceremonial magic.

CONE OF POWER — A cone of energy that is directed toward whatever or whomever. It is also used in Satanism.

CONJURATION — Is evoking or calling up the spirits to do what one commands them to do. They are confined to a triangle or circle drawn opn the floor. The triangle is a symbol of manifestation and the spirit force is to manifest itself inside the triangle or circle.

CONSECRATE — Simply means to make an object sacred. Many times the high priest will consecrate an object, animal, or human, before it is offered up in sacrifice.

COVEN — In non-traditional Satanism, covens will number 13 members. Normally when membership grows to more than 13, another coven will be formed. Traditional Satanists in most cases do not have covens. However, grottos can number from just a few to thousands, such as Anton LeVay's Church of Satan or the Temple of Set run by Michael Aquino.

CRESCENT — The time when the moon is in its waxing stage. It is a symbol of abundant growth as well as fertility.

CROSS — The Christian symbol of Christianity. It represents the Lord Jesus. To the Satanist, the cross is the symbol of Jesus Christ and for this reason, Satanists invert the cross, thus showing blasphemy toward Christianity.

CROWLEY, ALEISTER — One of the most diabolical individuals who ever lived. He was born in 1875, the year of the death of Eliphas Levi, who wrote several books on occultism. Crowley believed that he was a reincarnation of Levi. Many called Crowley the Beast, the Antichrist. He was thought to have made human sacrifices. He has inspired many others to get involved with the occult. In 1898 he joined the OTO (Ordo Templi Orientis) cult, also known as the Order of the Golden Dawn. He founded the Argenteum Astrum. Crowley's most famous book was *Magick in Theory and Practice,* published in 1929. He died in 1947.

CULT — A group of people who follow a charismatic leader who leads them to believe in him as some sort of diety. The term also describes practitioners of those beliefs.

CURSE — These are used only in black magic or sorcery, to inflict harm, destruction and even death. In order for any curse to work, a ritual must be performed and evil spirits summoned by invocations.

DAIMON — A demon, signified among pagan Greeks as an inferior deity.

DEMONOLOGY — The study of demons, what they are designated to do and how they are summoned, as well as what role they play with mankind today.

DEVIL, or DIABOLOS — The word means an accuser or slanderer. It is one of the names of Satan, who also is known as Lucifer.

DIABLERIE — One who deals with the devil or his demons, also one who deals in witchcraft or sorcery.

DIRECTIONS — The four elements are air, earth, fire and water and are symbolized in rituals.

ELEMENTS — In Satanism, there are four: bitom (fire), hcoma (water), exarp (air) and nanta (earth).

ELTZEN — The ruler of all the spirits of the north.

EQUINOX — This is a period of time when the sun crosses the equator. The spring equinox is March 21, while the fall equinox occurs on Sept. 22. On these days, the length of the daylight and dark hours are equal.

FULL MOON — When magical power is at its most powerful stage.

GOAT'S HEAD — Symbolic of Satan throughout the world. He is seen as the scapegoat for all bad things that occur. The goat's head is known by a number of names. For instance, the Goat of Mendez is a symbol of the black mass, according to the "Dictionary of Satanism," by Baskin.

GRIMOIRES — A collection of magical spells, incantations as well as rituals. The grimoires date back to medieval periods and are still used today in black magic.

HAND OF GLORY — The left hand of a person who has died. The hand is removed from the body, then pickled, embalmed or mummified. The practitioner then would place a candle in the palm of the hand. Sometimes candles are placed between the fingers. The ritual was used for protection against evil spirits.

HEAD — The powerhouse of the body. Those who practice the black arts consider the head to be source of all magical powers. For this reason, many human skulls are found on altars. Many Satanists believe that by eating the brain, one can receive powers from that person.

HEART — This is the center of life. Practitioners believe that by eating the heart of a victim, they can assume that victim's characteristics and obtain all of his power.

HEXAGRAM — A six-pointed star, also known as the Star of David, the hexagram is believed among those involved in the occult, to protect and control demons.

HORNED GOD — Part male and part goat, the horned god is a symbol of male sexuality.

HOST — Used in communion services, the host is symbolic of the Body of Christ. Those involved in the black arts often will try to steal a host that has been blessed by a Catholic priest. The host then is desecrated by several different ways, such as inserting it in the vagina of a female who is being used as an altar. Or the host can simply be thrown on the ground and trampled upon.

HOODOO — A combination of black magic and voodoo, it is used only to bring bad luck.

INCANTATION — Verbal spells recited by a practitioner in an effort to summon evil forces.

KALI — This word means black. Kali is a Hindu goddess who would accept only blood sacrifices. Such sacrifices still are being offered to this goddess today.

KEY OF SOLOMON — There have been two grimoires published: "The Greater Key of Solomon" and "The Lesser Key of Solomon." The latter gives detailed instructions on summoning the spirits.

LUCIFER — Morning Star; the archangel who protected the throne of God. Because of his pride, he was cast out and one-third of the angel population chose to follow him.

LUCIFERIANS — A Satanic sect active during the medieval period, this group sacrificed to demonic forces and felt that Lucifer was a brother to God and was wrongly expelled. Therefore they worshiped Lucifer.

MAGIC — There are two kinds of magic: white and black. White is used for purposes of good, while black magic is employed for destruction and harm.

MIDSUMMER'S EVE or ST. JOHN'S EVE — The festival for the beginning of summer is held on June 22.

NECROMANCY — The spirits of the dead are summoned, and they are asked to forecast the future or the secrets of the past.

NECROPHILIA — The act of having sexual intercourse with the dead.

NEOPHYTE — One who is about to go through the initiation into a coven.

NOVEMBER EVE — This is All Hallow's Eve, also called Sambain, which is Scottish Gaelic meaning All Hallow's Eve, occurs on Oct. 31.

OCCULT — A term which means hidden, secret or mysterious.

O.T.O. — Initials for Ordo Templi Orientis, a sect whose members practiced sexual magic. The order was founded by Karl Kellner. The infamous Aleister Crowley was a member who helped to revive O.T.O. in the middle 1920s.

ORIENS — Rules over all spirits of the East.

OWL — Among many cultures this bird is associated with death and evil powers.

PAGANS — Those who practice witchcraft. They worship nature as well as several gods.

PENTACLE — A five-pointed figure used as a magic symbol in rituals.

PENTAGRAM — A five-pointed star that is used in both the white crafts and the black crafts. When the star is inverted with two points up, it stands for black arts. When turned with a single point up, it symbolizes white magic. Pentagrams also are worn for protection.

RITUAL — A magical ceremony used in both white and black magic.

RUNES — A language, its name literally means secret. There are several types of runes.

SABBAT — A gathering of witches in honor of special dates.

SADISTIC — One who will deliberately torture or hurt any living creature.

SATAN — The angelic being created by the Christian God. He was an archangel who protected the throne of God. Because of his rebellious attitude, he was cast out of Heaven.

SATANIC — Refers to anything that pertains to Satan, which is evil.

SATANIC MASS (BLACK MASS) — The most perverted, blasphemous ritual that parodies the Christian communion or Catholic mass.

SEAL OF SOLOMON — Two interlocking triangles that form a hexagram. This seal is said to offer the greatest protection for the practitioner.

SHADOWS, BOOK OF — The personal book used and kept by the high priest within the coven or group. All of his rituals and spells are kept in this book. When the high priest dies, the book is destroyed. The book is also used by pagans.

SKYCLAD — Those who go nude. They believe that wearing clothes confines the powers of the body in working magic.

SOLOMON — The king of Israel who is said, by some involved in the occult, to have written several grimoires, one such called "The Lesser Keys of Solomon." Practitioners also use the Seals of Solomon.

SOLSTICE — Times of the year when the sun has no apparent northward or southward motion.

SPIRIT — When Satan was cast out of Heaven, one-third of the angel population chose to follow him. These are the spirits who are summoned during incantations.

SUCCUBUS — A female demonic force who copulates with human males.

VOODOO — A religion involving the practice of sorcery, participation in rituals with communication with spirits. Those who practice voodoo are heavily involved in fetishes and are extremely superstitious.

WALPURGIS NIGHT — May Day Eve, April 30, when "Missa Niger La Messe Noire" was first published. It was a book of the black mass, "a true and factual account of principal rituals of Satanic worship."

WARLOCK — A male witch.

WITCH — Can practice alone, or they can be a member of a coven.

WITCHCRAFT — The practice of the old religion which focuses on the goddess in her many forms: Hecate, Aphrodite, Asarte, Diana. Women play important roles in witchcraft.

Bibliography

C. Fried Dickason, Angels Elect and Evil, Moody Press, Chicago

Edred Thorsson, A Handbook of Rune Magic, Samuel Welser, Inc., York Beach, Maine

M. V. Devine, Brujeria: A Story of Mexican-American Folk Magic

Donna Rose, A Circle of Witches, Mi-World Publishing Company, Hialeah, Flordia, 1981

Marie Loveau, Black and White Magic—How to Perform Spells, Golden Eye, Torrance, California

Doreen Vallente, An ABC of Witchcraft—Past and Present

Anna Riva, Candle Burning Magic

Seleneicthon, Day Book of Ancient Spells, Mi-World Bookstore, 1983

E.A. Wallis Budge, Egyptian Magic, Dover Publications, New York

Gerald J. Schueler, Enochian Magic

Dolores Ashcroft-Nowicki, First Steps in Ritual, The Aquarian Press, 1982

Wade Baskin, Dictionary of Satanism, Philosophican Library, New York

Amber K., How To Organize a Coven, Circle Publications, Wisconsin, 1983

Montague Summers, History of Witchcraft and Demonology, Lyle Stuart Inc., New Jersey, 1956

Harry E. Wedeck, A Treasury of Witchcraft, Citadel Press

June Johns, King of the Witches, Coward-McCann, Inc., New York

Janet and Steward Farrar, Eight Sabbats of Witches, Robert Hale, London

Kurt Seligmann, The History of Magic and Occult

Colin Wilson, The Occult of History
Arthus Edward Waite, The Book of Ceremonial Magic, Bell Publishing Company, New York
Aubrey Melech, Missa Niger La Messe Noire, Sut Anubis Book Northhampton, England
Richard Cavendish, The Black Arts
Edmund M. Buczynski, Witchcraft Fact Book
Serge Bramly, Macumba, Avon Publishing Company
I.G. Edmonds, The King of Black Magic, Holt, Rinehart, and Winston, New York
Arthur Lyons, The Second Coming, Dodd, Mean and Company, New York
Rollo Ahmed, The Complete Book of Witchcraft, Paperback Library, New York
Sara Lyddon Morrison, The Modern Witches Spellbook, Lyle Stuard, Inc., Secaucus, New Jersey
Avon Books, Necronomicon, New York, New York
Migene Gonzalez-Wippler, Santeria African Magic in Latin America, Original Produts, Webster Avenue, Bronx, New York
Anton Szandor LaVey, The Satanic Rituals, Avon Books, New York, New York
Anton Szandor LaVey, The Satanic Bible, Avon Books, New York, New York
Migene Gonsalez, Rituals and Spells of Santeria, Original Products, Bronx, New York
E.M. Butler, Ritual Magic
Raymond Buckland, The Magick of Chant-O-Matic, Parker Publishing Company West Nyack, New York
Raymond Buckland, Practical Candleburning Rituals, Llewellyn Publication, St. Paul, Minnesota
Doifn, Nature Spirituality Cast a Magic Circle, Decatur, Georgia
Edmund M. Buczynski, Witchcraft Fact Book, Magickal Childe Publishing Inc., New York, New York

Keith Muray, Ancient Rites & Ceremonies, Tutor Press, Toronto, Canada

Raymond Buckland, The Complete Book of Saxon Witchcraft, Samuel Weiser, New York, New York

Index

216

217

219

The Authors

Tom Wedge, a former juvenile probation officer with the Logan County (OH) Common Pleas Court, is a consultant to law enforcement agencies throughout the country on the subjects of Satanism and occult and ritualistic crimes. He lectures extensively and has appeared on major tv and radio talk shows. He and his wife, Brenda, reside in Columbus, Ohio.

Robert Powers is a freelance writer with more than three decades' experience as a journalist.

Cover artwork by Rich Hendrus.

Also from Calibre Press

Books for Law Enforcement

STREET SURVIVAL: TACTICS FOR ARMED
ENCOUNTERS
  by Special Agent Ronald Adams, Lt. Thomas McTernan,
  Charles Remsberg

THE TACTICAL EDGE: SURVIVING HIGH-RISK PATROL
  by Charles Remsberg

ROADSIDE SOBRIETY TESTS: A POLICE OFFICER'S
GUIDE TO MAKING DRUNK DRIVING ARRESTS
STAND UP IN COURT
  by James Whitmore

Videocassettes

ULTIMATE SURVIVORS: WINNING AGAINST
INCREDIBLE ODDS
  hosted by William Shatner; produced and directed by
  Dennis Anderson

SURVIVING EDGED WEAPONS
  produced and directed by Dennis Anderson

**For a free catalog of unique law enforcement books,
videos and other products, contact:**

Calibre Press, Inc.
666 Dundee Road
Suite 1607
Northbrook, IL 60062-2760

(800) 323-0037
(708) 498-5680
Fax: (708) 498-6869

**Special discounts available for group purchases.
Dealer inquiries invited.**